Also by Charles Ortleb

Iron Peter: A Year in the Mythopoetic Life of New York City

The Closing Argument: A Shocking Courtroom Novella

Silence, Exile, and Cunning: A Trilogy

The Last Lovers on Earth

Stories from Dark Times

Charles Ortleb

Rubicon Media
New York City

The Last Lovers on Earth: Stories from Dark Times

Published in the United States by Rubicon Media,

Copyright © 1999 by Charles Ortleb

First Rubicon Media Edition: August, 1999

PRINTED IN THE UNITED STATES OF AMERICA

Contents

"Everywhere, on billboards, in the newspapers, on the screen, we encountered the revolting and insipid picture of ourselves that our suppressors wanted us to accept."
—*Jean-Paul Sartre*
The Republic of Silence

"The horrible can be not only ludicrous, but downright funny."
—*Hannah Arendt*
Eichmann in Jerusalem

"The one weapon against which Robespierre was helpless then struck him down: Laughter."
—*Simon Schama*
Citizens

The Retraction

The parents started to feel a little nervous when their son called ahead and said that he wanted to sit down for a talk with them as soon as he got home from work. He had sounded edgy and they both remembered the last time he had anxiously requested a heart-to-heart with them. Their lives hadn't been the same since. What could it be now?

When he arrived home he quickly bounded up the stairs, took a shower, and donned his signature outfit of khaki shorts and a white T-shirt. He asked his mother to make them all double vodka and tonics and to wait for him in the sun room. That he seemed to think they all needed such strong drinks was disturbing.

When their handsome, sole offspring entered the glass-enclosed room, the sun was just setting, and there was a soft, evocative light in the room that was kind to his mother and father's weathered features. For the mother, who had already gulped down half her drink, a kind of incipient numbness had set in, perhaps as protection for what her son might be about to say.

The last time they'd had a talk that was set up like this, she had ended up loaded and in tears. Her husband had carried her to bed. She was now a little angry. She was getting too old for surprises. She thought people should be careful about what they say to anyone over fifty. She anxiously focused her eyes on her son.

"How was the office, son?" asked the father.

"Disgusting."

"Well, maybe you should look around," said the father.

"Maybe they'll fire me, and I could collect. My nerves are shot. I can't make cold calls like that all day long."

"Well, son, most jobs involve some selling, some calling," said the father.

"If it was something else, maybe I wouldn't be so frustrated. But people just don't seem to want to buy cake decorating equipment by phone."

"Maybe you could go back to cooking school," the mother chimed in.

"That was a disaster," he said. "I just need to find some time to figure things out."

The father, somewhat relieved, said, "So that's what you wanted to talk to us about—your career?"

"No," he responded.

"Oh," the mother sighed.

"No, it's bigger than that."

"Well, shoot then, son."

"I really hate breaking things like this to you. You've both been through so much. I feel so guilty for what I've already put you through."

"It's a terminal illness isn't it?" the mother blurted out, with her hand over her eyes.

"No, mother, I'm in perfect health."

"Your mother always likes to jump to the worst conclusions. Well, what is it then?" asked the father, his voice cracking a little.

"I'm not gay."

"Oh, Jesus, Mary, and Joseph!" screamed the mother.

"Now wait just a minute, young man," said the father.

"I made a terrible mistake coming out to you last year. It turns out that I'm not gay. I'm sorry."

The father fell back into the chaise lounge but then abruptly sat up.

"Let's all take a deep breath. I don't want anyone to panic," said the father. He always liked to assume the role of the captain at sea.

"I should have known it," the mother said.

"That's what you said when I told you I was gay."

"I should have known it when you didn't try to write a gay novel. That should have been the giveaway. I looked for first drafts in your socks drawer, but I never found a single page."

"Well, I'm glad to hear that you've been looking through my things."

"I was only hoping to find condoms," said the mother. "Your father and I are always worried about safe sex."

"I'm sorry I've made you worry about anything."

"This is a little crazy son. Are you gonna get us both drunk next year and change your mind and tell us you're gay again? Is this a revolving door we're all in?"

"No, Dad. This is real. This is sure. I just made a terrible mistake and wasted a year of your life. You've both been so supportive about this. I'm very grateful to both of you for that."

"You mean we won't be riding on the 'Parents of Gays' float this year?"

"No, you don't have to do anything. You can stay home or go to the mall or play golf. You don't have to fight for gay rights. I have all the rights I need, because I'm not gay."

"Son, are you absolutely sure about this? After all, you are very effeminate."

"I know Dad, but I'm not gay. I'm just an effeminate heterosexual male. I'm a flaming straight, I guess. You're not exactly John Wayne either, Dad."

"The more I think about it, though, you really might be wrong this time," said the mother.

"Why?"

"You used to dress up in my clothes when you were a little boy."

"I still do, mother. But I'm not gay."

"You will still do my hair for me every Friday evening, won't you?"

"Yes, Mother."

"What are we supposed to tell everyone?"

"That it was all a misunderstanding. That I'm not gay."

"We can't tell your grandparents," said the mother.

"Why not?"

"Because they'll be so confused. They'll think we're all crazy."

"But all of our friends have become so sensitive and understanding. Son, I hope you know what widespread repercussions this is going to have," said the father.

"Do you really have to guilt-trip me?"

"Will we still have brunches on Sunday, son?" asked the mother as she looked out the window at a black bird in the distant sky. It seemed to connect to the tiny forlorn feeling that was flying around inside her.

"I don't see why not," replied the son.

"I'm going to miss the Parents of Gays meetings. I got so good at comforting mothers who broke down about their gay children," said the mother. "They're all going to think that we're in some kind of denial. They may send out a team of parents for an intervention. Your father was great with the other fathers, especially the distraught ones. He'd pat them on the back and say, 'Chin up, pal. This gay thing is not such a big deal. It's just a special buddy relationship, after all, don't you think?' It always did the trick."

The mother decided right then and there not to second-guess her son's sexual nature, but it did seem to be changing on an annual basis.

"I never thought I'd say this," the father said, "but it's very strange to suddenly not be the parents of a gay."

In the weeks and months that followed, they tiptoed around the giant hole where the gay son had been in their lives. One son had died and another one had risen from his grave. It was very unsettling, for in some ways, over the last twelve months, the father and mother had thrown themselves so aggressively into understanding and defending their son, that each in their own way had become just a little bit gay.

Once they had gotten over the initial shock, they adopted the role of supportive parents with a vengeance. Not only had they immediately joined Parents of Gays, but they also had a big coming out party for their son. They invited all their friends and relatives. With a few exceptions, everyone had been team players and the party turned out to be one of the liveliest they had ever given. A couple of the son's cousins even chose to come out as trendy bisexuals at the party. But now they were faced with the question of what to do with the presents. The mother insisted that they should just follow the same etiquette used for bridal showers when the wedding is cancelled.

The coming out gift they were most concerned about was from the mother's parents. The grandparents were wealthy liberals who lived on the Upper West Side of Manhattan and they gave their newly gay grandson a brand new BMW. They didn't want to be outdone by their friends with gay grandchildren. The mother said the grandparents would be furious if the son tried to give the car back.

It was difficult to tell who took the retraction hardest, the mother or the father. The father sheepishly told some of his closest friends that his son might not be gay, just to see what the general reaction would be. The father sensed that his best golfing buddy thought that the son had simply gone back into the closet, which was just fine with him. Most of the father's friends didn't much like the son anyway.

The mother took more time to spread the word in her social circle because, frankly, she hadn't had many friends before her son came out. Most of her phone friends now were mothers of gays, lesbians, or bisexuals. Much of the mother's day had consisted of gossiping with other mothers about the problems of their gay children. Just keeping track of everyone's relationships was a full-time job. The mother kept a chart of all the friends' sons and daughters, along with the names of lovers and ex-lovers. There were so many names crossed out and so many arrows going in all directions that the chart looked like a map of a football coach's wildest strategies. It had become a totally engrossing and surprising occupation, and as odd as it seemed, the whole enterprise had made the mother feel more alive than she had felt in years. When you have a son who is a wee bit swishy, after years of thinking the worst, and putting every kind of spin on your own intuitions, it comes as a peculiar kind of relief when he tells you that he is gay. But that weird relief was now history.

After the son had come out, the parents' calendar was full of events that were supportive of gays and lesbians. They quickly found themselves attending weekly meetings and volunteering for all kinds of gay organizations. They subscribed to the *Advocate* and several other gay publications. They sent a generous check to the National Gay and Lesbian Task Force. Within a few months of the son's coming out, the thought struck them that they were doing more for the gay cause than their son was. They found themselves bowling with the siblings of gays and lesbians, hiking in the Catskills with the uncles and aunts of gays and lesbians, attending Broadway openings with the nephews and nieces of gays and lesbians, and perhaps most surprisingly, they spent one weekend helping a bald lesbian put together a cabaret act with her father in their garage. The parents had even joined a Parents of Gays bridge club and had subsequently come to the conclusion that may gays and lesbians have card sharks for parents. (That said, they enjoyed the evenings and hoped they would still be welcome.)

They had been determined not to let their son down.

They had wanted him to know that their love was unconditional. The gay movement had become their movement. They were not political people. The anti-war movement had passed them both by. From an activist point of view, they were letting the environment and the ozone layer go to hell. What they had thought was their son's struggle for gay civil rights had become their lifeline to the public square. They had become citizens in the most robust manner; they marched and they protested and they carried around signs that were simple but defiant, signs that said things like "Our Son is Gay and We Like Him That Way," and most outrageously, "We Wish We Were Gay." Until their son had come out, the annual Gay Pride Parade had always appeared to them as some kind of lurid freak show, but when they found themselves in the middle of it, on one of the colorful floats with disco dancers in G-strings cavorting around them, they suddenly were full of empathy for all living creatures, straight and gay. The event lifted their spirits and seemed to connect them to freedom fighters everywhere. This had truly become their cause. By suddenly not being gay, their son had taken away some of the meaning of their lives. They thought about the possibility of starting an organization for parents of nongays, but the prospect seemed awkward and unwieldy.

As the reality of their son not being gay sank in, things began to change in their household. For some reason, after their son came out, the mother had started to keep fresh flowers around. The son had not asked for them, but it seemed appropriate. Now the vases were empty. With the exception of *Lesbian Homes and Gardens*, the mother let all the other gay subscriptions expire.

Both parents found themselves doing things they couldn't quite explain. The symptoms of some mild, mysterious depression began to materialize. The father began to do something he hadn't done since he was a kid: stutter. And sometimes, when he was alone in the car driving to work, he would start to sob uncontrollably for no reason at all. Instead of getting closer to his son, he found himself spending more time alone. At first he thought that his son not being gay meant that they would start doing more guy things together. He thought he should show his son more about the intricacies of fixing a car, or take him to the country club to play golf, or even do something they had never done—go on a hunting trip together and kill something.

The mother found herself talking to herself more. She tried to keep up some of the relations with the mothers of gays she had befriended, but it just wasn't the same. In the colorful circle that had formed around her, there was an unspoken disdain for parents who didn't have any gay children. For the first time in her life, she was sorry that they had decided to be prudent and have only one baby.

The following autumn the mother got in her car and took a trip to the outskirts of their town to dispose of the secret thing she had created shortly after her son had come out. Subsequent to joining Parents of Gays, the mother and father had accompanied parents from around the nation to visit the AIDS Quilt in Washington. The AIDS Quilt was bigger than a hundred football fields and consisted of panels from all over America sewn together to create a mesmerizing and gut-wrenching image. Each panel represented one person who had died of AIDS. The leaders of Parents of Gays had insisted that the AIDS Quilt was a very important thing for every parent of a gay to see. Even though the mother and father were not the parents of a dead gay and did not know anyone who had died of AIDS, they found themselves sniffling and trying to console the relatives and friends who were overcome with grief as they gazed upon the colorful sea of the departed.

When she returned home, the mother did more than take to wearing a red ribbon around the house. She didn't only warn her son about the dangers of unprotected sex.

Wanting to prepare herself for the absolute worst, she clandestinely began to work on her son's panel for the AIDS Quilt, just in case. It had not escaped her attention that many of the panels were expertly crafted acts of love and affection. Some of the panels, even though they were only a few square feet, looked like Martha Stewart or Vera Wang had created them. Some parents and friends had captured entire life stories in the panels. The taste represented by many of them was exquisite. Some had expensive jewels sewn into them. Some had teddy bears or Ken dolls affixed. Surprisingly, a few had soccer shoes, footballs, or baseball mitts expertly attached, which especially got to the fathers. Each panel tried to embody the lost essence of a gay man. Each panel was the expression of the tortured and imploring hands of friends or parents reaching up to heaven. The mother was worried that if her son died of AIDS, the grief would be so overwhelming that she wouldn't be able to concentrate enough to construct a panel for the AIDS Quilt that wouldn't embarrass their family and friends. So she surreptitiously began working on a panel for her son so that she would always be prepared for the worst. She didn't want her son's potential AIDS Quilt panel to look like they had just stopped and bought it at a Kmart on their way to Washington.

During the days that followed their visit to the Quilt, when her husband and son were at work, the mother began to put together the most meaningful tribute to the memory of her not-yet-dead son. She crept into her son's bedroom and opened the sliding door to his extremely cluttered closet and explored its dark recess, as if she were extending her arms into her son's past itself. From the closet she plucked items that summed up his life and brought nostalgic tears to her eyes. His first baton from when he tried to be a majorette. A tiny feather boa from his first Halloween in drag. White gloves he insisted on wearing with his Cub Scout uniform. A small blond wig from when his third grade class tried to do *Follies*. As she clandestinely removed these items from her son's bedroom, she felt like she had a transcendent armful of her gay son's precious time on earth.

The mother pensively wove the items into an imagistic narrative about her son's life. Of course, she had to leave part of the panel unfinished. The date of her son's birth on the panel was followed only by a dash. She never showed the panel to the father and she was always terrified that the son might find it and never forgive her.

Presently, the panel was next to her on the passenger side of the front seat of her car in a large black garbage bag. The mother wore dark sunglasses. She prayed that none of her neighbors would by chance be at the city dump that day. When she arrived at the dump she used a large pair of shearing scissors to cut up the panel into several small pieces. As she drove back home, the memento of the AIDS death her son had not died lay beneath old egg cartons and rusty cans of V8.

At home there was still one secret to dispose of. At the back of her own closet, behind shoes her husband would never wear again, was a large cardboard box. In that box were hundreds of old newspaper clippings. Following her son's announcement that he was gay, almost every day she began to cut stories out of the newspaper. Some days there were two or three stories to clip. Because her son was gay, she began to worry about every gay person in the world. Whenever there was a story about a gay person who was beaten up, murdered, dismembered, or discriminated against, the mother clipped it. In her box there were clippings about gay people who had been stabbed, shot, beaten with baseball bats, even thrown from bridges. Gays who had been beheaded or stoned in other lands. In one fundamentalist country, they toppled brick walls upon gay people. The story that had gotten to the mother more than any other involved a woman in the American Northwest.

She had taken a retarded gay man into her home in order to protect him from violent bigots during a period when their redneck county was in a frenzy over an anti-gay referendum in their state—one that was going to pass. When a local group of bullies found out that the retarded gay man was staying at the woman's house, they firebombed it, killing both their target and the good Samaritan.

Subsequently, for many weeks the mother woke up in the middle of the night, struggling in the flames with the woman and the gay retarded man. One by one, every gay person that she read about who was harmed not only became one of her concerns, they became one of her children. Her motherhood expanded out of her body, through the roof of her house, and spread across the sky for as far as the heart could see.

Like a surprising number of housewives in America, the mother had been a closet atheist, at least before her son came out. The accumulating clippings in her cardboard box began to weigh so heavily on the mother's psyche that she had what can only be called a mini-theological breakdown. Or you could say that her soul had a stroke. One night, out of the overwhelming fear for her son suddenly came a new faith and a god she could pray to. There just had to be a god to protect her gay son from everything that was happening in her box of newspaper clippings. Her longing for a god to protect her son was so ferocious and desperate that sometimes she felt palpitations in her chest. She prayed to her new gay-friendly god for her son constantly. It was the kind of naked-unto-god extreme praying that soldiers do in foxholes next to dying buddies. It was the only thing that gave her peace. Her gay son had taken his mother on a journey into the deepest mysteries within.

But now she was proceeding with the box of her people and her children toward the patio in the backyard.

There she removed the grate from the barbecue grill and, after filling it with charcoal and sprinkling the coals with starter fluid, she poured all of the newspaper clippings onto the black mound and struck a match. Within minutes the world she thought she would spend the rest of her days fighting for went up in flames. The clipping about the woman and the retarded gay man in the Northwest was the first to turn into ashes.

There was a new quiet in her house when she went back inside. There would be no more dark nights of fear and prayer. The poor souls on her barbecue outside would have to fend for themselves. God. Politics. Friendship. Commitment. What an odyssey it had been. But now it was over. Her son had changed tribes, and she and her husband felt the sad duty to follow him once again. She hoped their son was happy even though, like most sons, he had no idea what he had done.

Ex-gayville, Connecticut

Beth and I had been talking seriously about settling down in Ex-gayville, Connecticut for several months. We were still a little shaky in our ex-gayness and ex-lesbianism, but we thought that we could make a lot more progress in Ex-gayville than on the Upper West Side of Manhattan.

We had both recently experienced some momentary relapses, and we felt that we were being challenged too frequently by our liberal environment. And we both had been imbibing a little too much. The ban on liquor in Ex-gayville struck us as just the discipline we needed to embrace our incipient ex-gay lifestyle.

The night I got really drunk and started singing the Streisand-Summer hit duet "Enough is Enough," doing both voices was probably when I hit bottom. The next morning we called a real estate agent in Ex-gayville.

We were full of hopes for a new life in the sleepy Connecticut town as we drove out of Manhattan.

"Matt, I pray that they don't have any softball or volleyball teams there," she said.

"Oh, don't worry," I said. "I'm sure they've cleaned the whole place up. I've heard that they even have a city ordinance against women's golf."

"Thank God," said Beth. "My hair doesn't look too short, does it?"

"Not at all, honey. No one would know."

"Know what?"

"Know where you're...where you're coming from."

"You mean know I used to be a big ol' dyke?"

"Beth, you know that Dr. Frick and the group have suggested that it doesn't help either of us solidify our ex-gayness if you talk that way."

"I'm sorry, honeybun," she said.

"That's more like it."

"Did you have to wear that shirt?" asked Beth. "You look like you should be marching at the front of a Gay Pride parade."

"Boy, are you in a bad mood, Beth. I saw Regis Philbin wear a shirt like this last week."

"Now there's a macho icon for you."

"Beth, you're exhibiting unresolved anxiety about change. Dr. Frick said this would happen."

"Go ahead and say it, Matt. My lesbianism is acting up."

"I haven't said that to you in months, sweetie."

When we arrived in Ex-gayville, we were escorted around town by an ex-lesbian real estate agent named Ethel Perkins, who had brokered half the houses in the Hamptons in her prior life when she was a very active lesbian. There were quite a few available houses in Ex-gayville because lately, for some reason no one could put their finger on, there had been a larger than usual number of relapses in the community. The real estate broker joked that backsliding was good for her business, but Beth didn't quite see the humor in it.

Ethel the ex-lesbian showed us a Cape Cod, which I immediately nixed because it reminded me too much of Provincetown.

"I know just what you need," said Ethel. "I have just the right ranch for you two ex-gay lovebirds."

"Not too many windows," I insisted. I had a deathly fear that someone would look into our bedroom sometime and see what a dreadful, complicated mess we made out of sex.

"I'm sorry, but all houses have some windows," she replied.

Beth and I immediately fell in love with the place. We thought we had found the Promised Land of our ex-gayness. I could imagine puttering around the house and fixing things to keep my mind off my former life. And Beth could see herself baking up a storm in the large kitchen. We wanted to have children, but weren't quite sure how we were going to pull that off. But if in fact we did, there were two little bedrooms for our ex-gay children. We made a down payment that day, and within two months we were moving all of our sophisticated Manhattan designer furniture into our ranch in Ex-gayville.

The welcome from our new ex-gay and ex-lesbian neighbors could not have been warmer. Most of the men had two names, their prior gay name and their new Ex-gayville one. Our next door neighbor Ted was the former Miss Coco Puff of New Orleans. Joe, the husky guy across the street, was once Miss Big Thing in Harlem. (Yes, Ex-gayville was very integrated.) Ted's wife, Alice, was the former Motor Mike of the West Village leather lesbian scene. Joe's wife, Cerise, used to be known in the lesbian bars of Atlanta as Thunder Thighs.

We were given a very pleasant cookies-and-lemonade reception at Joe and Cerise's. I didn't dare ask for a little shot of something in the lemonade, because, as I said, booze was strictly forbidden in Ex-gayville. It was considered to be the water from the river of gay temptation, a definite no-no. One counselor had said to us that the drunker one gets, the gayer one gets. I couldn't argue with that.

We did our very best to fit in. Like all the other ex-lesbian women, Beth stayed home every day and cleaned and cooked and watched *Oprah*. This was quite a change for Beth, because when I first met her, cleaning usually meant putting everything in her apartment in five or six piles.

Beth took to cleaning our new home with a vengeance. She washed all the floors every day and our house was so dust-free you could have assembled a computer chip in any room. She even took apart the clock and toaster and cleaned every moving part. I marveled at her transformation the night I pulled into the driveway and found her cleaning the garage with a toothbrush.

The competition among the ex-lesbians to be the best housewife was fierce, and Beth got right into the fray and tried to claim first prize. She quickly achieved the reputation in the neighborhood of being the most ambitious cookie baker. Maybe it was that remark by Hillary Clinton about not staying home and baking cookies for her man that got all the ex-lesbians going. Or maybe it was the questionable research that some Ex-gayville academic had done showing that Sappho never baked anything. I don't know what it was, but for some reason the air in Ex-gayville was always fragrant with freshly baked cookies.

Beth baked far more cookies than the two of us could ever eat. I took cookies to the office. We gave tins of them away to the children in the neighborhood. I even gave cookies regularly to the toll booth operator on the morning commute. Every night we had cookies for dessert and then later for a midnight snack. It was strange seeing a woman who didn't have children constantly baking cookies. Beth gave so many cookies away on our block that several mothers complained that she was causing eating disorders in their children. There were several bulimics in the neighborhood.

Actually, all of the children in Ex-gayville were a little weird. Many of them had a spaced-out, faraway look in their eyes. I also noticed that the children were always a little nervous and they didn't seem to know what they were supposed to do or say. Maybe it was because they were raised by parents who were in a constant journey out of their gay and lesbianness. Conversations in Ex-gayville went by in a blur. People spoke in wary sound bites. Everyone seemed to be afraid to stand still. The only child who seemed at peace with herself was Ted and Alice's little Vanessa. She was an unusually calm child, but Vanessa also had a little morbid streak. She believed she had the gift of prophecy and she was always foretelling the deaths of neighbors. On one occasion, little Vanessa told Beth and myself that we were going to die soon.

Beth and I looked horrified at her parents, but Vanessa's mother merely shrugged her shoulders, saying, "Look, we can't control her gifts. What can I tell you? She says that to everyone and sometimes she gets lucky."

Many of the children in Ex-gayville eventually had troubled adolescences. It was not unusual for some of the friskier teens to act out the issues of ex-gayness by spray-painting graffiti like "Mr. Olsen has a lisp," or "Mrs. Patterson still eats pussy," on the sides of the houses in our highly sensitive community. And making matters worse was the fact that the graffiti was often right on the money.

In such a world, I had to stay on my toes and keep my ex-gay nose to the grindstone. I had already cut off my ponytail and ditched the single earring. I continued actively working on my ex-gay makeover. My voice was getting deeper, my walk more manly. For the most part the word "fabulous" was exiled from my vocabulary except for very special occasions. I tried to glance at the sports page every day, even though my hands perpetually strayed to arts and fashion. I took the draconian step of ditching all my Brad Pitt movies. I took to wearing a fedora and occasionally smoking a pipe. My cynical next door neighbor was not very helpful. He barely concealed a giggle whenever he saw me in a smoking jacket lighting up my pipe.

"Ted, do you have to sabotage my emerging masculinity?" I once asked him indignantly.

"I didn't mean no harm, Miss Scarlet," he responded.

"Ted, you could get thrown out of Ex-gayville for a crack like that."

Luckily for him, there was a rather endearing amount of loyalty among the ex-gay men in the neighborhood. We often had to cover for each other's *faux pas*. Ex-gayville men didn't tend to turn each other in for such infractions. The loyalty was ironic in that it resembled the loyalty we felt when we had been gay and in the closet.

The men in the neighborhood often gathered together to watch baseball and football. We were supposed to be bonding without cruising. We all watched each other watching these games, to see who was looking too closely at the players' asses while trying not to do so ourselves.

Near the end of our first year in Ex-gayville I began to notice subtle changes in Beth that soon grew into dramatic ones. Some nights in the middle of dinner, she would get up to clean something or wash a floor and then return to the table.

When I questioned her one night about this strange behavior, she snapped at me.

"I want this house to be perfect for you. And this is the thanks I get? Twenty questions?"

"I'm sorry, Beth."

She left the table and went to bed. I sat eating the rest of my dinner even though I could hear her sobbing into her pillow. It sounded like someone weeping millions of miles away.

When I finished my meal I did all the dishes myself and went into our bedroom as though nothing had happened. I undressed in the dark, listening to Beth mourning in the darkness on her side of the bed.

I knew that our relationship was really not on the right track to complete ex-gayness. I could see that we were taking our frustrations out on each other. Beth must have known what I was thinking, because all of a sudden, from her side of the bed came the words, "I bet every marriage in Ex-gayville is a marriage from Hell."

It was one of the few times I really felt close to her. I pulled her over to my side of the bed and we were uncharacteristically affectionate toward each other before we fell asleep.

Beth didn't give up on our ex-gay marriage, and neither did I. But the more she tried to throw herself into her role, the more bizarre her behavior became.

Between Thanksgiving and Christmas that year, she started spending more and more time watching television and less and less time cooking and cleaning. And she watched the same thing over and over and over: episodes of *Leave It to Beaver.*

One night, when I arrived home, she greeted me at the door in her apron. After giving me a big kiss, she called me "Ward."

At first I was amused, but when she began calling me "Ward" all the time, I sensed something bigger was happening.

She had videotaped all of the *Leave It to Beaver* episodes and played them nonstop day and night. She would sit staring at the set, only periodically getting up to imitate June Cleaver. She dusted things exactly like June Cleaver. She sent for a retro fashion catalog and bought clothes that looked exactly like June Cleaver's. She began to talk and gesticulate like June Cleaver all day long. Whenever I protested, she ignored me or just said, "Oh, Ward, run up and see if Wally and the Beaver are washing up for dinner."

I didn't know what to do or say. I couldn't tell the neighbors and there was no one I dared tell at the office. I was thinking about calling her parents, but I didn't want to give them the satisfaction. They never believed our marriage would last in the first place.

Things came to a head the week before Christmas when I came home and found Beth in a state of total hysteria.

She screamed at me as soon as I walked in. "Ward, I found a bra in Beaver's underwear drawer."

"Beth, calm down."

"Ward, I knew it. The Beaver is a lesbian."

"Beth, the Beaver is a boy. I mean, there's no Beaver. We don't have a Beaver or an anything."

"And Ward, I have some terrible news about Wally."

"Beth, there is no Wally."

"Ward, I caught Wally disco-dancing in the basement in the nude. And he was wearing a cockring."

'Beth, we don't have a basement. Or a Wally."

"Ward, I think Wally's gay. The Beaver's a lesbian, and Wally's living the gay lifestyle."

"Beth, I think you need help. I think we need help."

I ran to the phone and called her parents.

Her nasty younger brother answered the phone. I told him vaguely what was happening, and he predictably responded in a snide way: "Well, that's quite a marriage you two have got going there. I bet she's still a lezzie."

"Calvin, let me talk to your parents."

Within a few hours, her parents had made the drive from Manhattan to Ex-gayville. While Beth was marching around the house screaming at Wally and the Beaver, I packed a big bag of what I thought were her favorite clothes. She was screaming so loud that I was afraid the neighbors could all hear.

At the top of her lungs she shouted, "WALLY AND THE BEAVER, YOU MUST STOP BEING GAY AND LESBIAN THIS MINUTE! WE'LL ALL BE KILLED!" She kept screaming it over and over.

As soon as they walked through the front door, Beth ran up to her parents and said, "Mother and Father, Wally and the Beaver are gay and lesbian, and it's all Ward's fault."

Luckily, they still knew how to deal with their daughter. Of course, they gave me dirty looks, as if I had done something terrible to her.

They took the bag I packed and got Beth out to the

car without her even looking back. Oddly, I felt an incredible sense of relief as I watched the car disappear into the night with my ex-lesbian wife and perhaps the last remnants of my marriage. Her parents had always desperately wanted her to be like June Cleaver, and now their wish had come true.

I was thankful that I had buried a bottle of vodka in the backyard. I went outside, dug it up with my bare hands and went into the kitchen and made the biggest and strongest screwdriver that has ever been made in violation of the sobriety rules of Ex-gayville. I was risking the total loss of control that they were always warning us about in the town meetings of Ex-gayville, but I didn't care. I drank the screwdriver like it was my first mother's milk. I didn't know what was going to become of me. Could I be an ex-gay without an ex-lesbian wife? Would I be asked to leave Ex-gayville? It was a forgiving community, but it had its rules. As I pondered my future, the screwdriver took my mind down a dozen different paths.

I guess I should have been sitting there fretting about Beth, but I suddenly cared only about myself, and that was making me feel surprisingly happy. I don't know what made me do it, but I gave in to a spontaneous urge to take off my clothes. I took them off, all of them, and threw them all over the room as if they were bad, evil things. When I was completely naked I started dancing around the living room. Wally wasn't dancing naked in our home, I was. I felt freer than I had in my entire life.

I made myself another drink and chug-a-lugged it. I was utterly alone, but I felt totally alive. I didn't know what to do next. I started walking around the house. I paced and paced, faster and faster, from room to room. I raced throughout our home like an animal on fire in a cage. Then I did something incredibly reckless.

I walked from window to window and stared out. I was completely nude. It was crazy and dangerous, but I

29

couldn't help it. I stood in the nude at each window and stared out into the darkness of Ex-gayville. Anyone on the block could have seen me standing in my glorious altogether at the window.

The really surprising thing was that I was not alone. I could see Joe standing across the street at his window, nude. And when I ran to a window on the side of the house, I could see that Ted was standing naked at his window next door. Up and down the street I could see a naked man standing at a window in every home. In the shadows of Ex-gayville, a couple of them even appeared to have erections. Their faces were contorted, and they all looked like they were screaming or roaring soundlessly through the double panes of glass. I thought, my God—could this really have been going on every night since we moved here?

It was the most uncanny thing I had ever seen, all the men of Ex-gayville standing in the nude at windows, peering desperately into the distance, searching the overcast sky for the moon, or a star, or a hand, and finding nothing, nothing at all.

Bruschetta on the Beach

The city glistened in Eddie's eyes like the gates of heaven. He was seeing it for the first time through tears of relief and joy. What was left in the trail of dark and sickening smoke behind the Greyhound bus was not just the industrial countryside of New Jersey, but two very difficult formative decades that would probably have discouraged hope in Pollyanna herself. But not Eddie. He would never have made it this close to Oz without his own persistent and mysterious inner reserve of optimism. You would never know that behind him lay twenty years of not being wanted or loved.

There was nobody and nothing waiting for Eddie in New York City. His only real possessions were his dreams and his willingness to work hard and earn his way into a gay community that he hoped would heal every hurt, and correct every injustice in his past. He knew that he could find himself and be himself only among his own people. They would be the supportive family he never had.

As the bus emerged from the Hudson Tunnel, he waved to total strangers on the street as though they had been waiting for him to arrive all their lives.

Even though he had little money and only two years of junior college to his name, the high spirits of the late Seventies effervesced inside Eddie. It seemed like the best time in history to be gay. He practically expected the streets to be paved with beefcake. Eddie looked around the Port Authority terminal as though he anticipated some kind of immigration committee to greet him with gay clothes, a gay job, and gay housing. But not a soul seemed to take any interest in the fact that the gay population of Manhattan had just been definitively increased by one. Even though there was no gay Welcome Wagon awaiting him, Eddie never stopped smiling as he found his way to a cheap hotel. He was full of the zest of one who has just liberated himself from dark times.

Eddie was industrious and within a week he got one of the first requisite jobs that gay emigrants obtain on their way to finding their water level in the city. He felt filled with possibility when he took a part-time position as a dog walker, but soon realized that he would not be able to survive on the meager wages. He then began a series of lateral career moves and dips through jobs like making feather boas and handing out flyers for gay bathhouses. He finally found a job that paid a living wage as a D.J. in a bowling alley. Disco was very big then, and Eddie thought that being able to play records carefully, dance energetically, and wave a tambourine enthusiastically in the air while drawing a paycheck was about as good as it gets.

Eddie hoped that someone who owned one of the popular gay dance clubs would happen to stop in at the bowling alley and be impressed by his musical selections. But not too many club owners seemed to be into bowling in those days. People were taking so many drugs that they didn't have time to bowl.

Eddie found a little rent-controlled apartment on the Lower East Side that he could barely afford. It was a very run-down building. Some apartments had blankets hanging as doors. He fixed his place up so he wouldn't be embarrassed to bring home a potential lover.

To say that Eddie was ordinary looking would be considered a major compliment. God had kind of doubled up on Eddie, because not only was he a member of a much maligned minority group, but he was also as ugly as sin. Eddie knew that if he were to attract someone, he would have to win them over with something other than superficial beauty. He was no genius either, so he couldn't expect to attract the type who love people for their minds. As he inventoried himself, Eddie decided that his most valuable asset was his smile. While it couldn't be described as winning, his smile was overwhelmingly optimistic. Eddie hoped that there was someone out there who desperately needed encouragement, for emotional support was what Eddie knew he could offer a lover night and day.

Eddie cleaned his apartment very carefully every evening before venturing out into the bars to look for Mr. Anybody. He knew that enough in life was stacked up against him without him bringing home a stranger only to have him discover that Eddie was a major slob. Maybe someone would be attracted to him because he could see that he would be an excellent housekeeper. Before he left for the evening, he also made sure that there were plenty of impressive snacks, wine, and beer in the refrigerator. He could keep the right guy well fed.

It didn't matter how clean Eddie's apartment was, or what was in the fridge, because night after night, he trekked home alone. This was the time when people were sleeping with anything that wasn't tied down, and some things that were. But not Eddie. Some invisible hand in the universe kept sex and love at a constant distance from Eddie. Even New Year's Eve of 1979—when virtually everybody in Manhattan got drunk and slept with a stranger—found Eddie in bed alone as he greeted the new decade. There was an expression used in the bars and discos that year, "The It Boy," which described the lucky kind of fellow whom everyone wanted to date at that moment. In many ways Eddie seemed destined to be "The Not-It boy," of his era. But he never lost hope that his luck would change. He just kept smiling.

People didn't avoid Eddie completely. Many gay men actually befriended him because he looked so helpful. And he was the kind of person you could always talk happily to at the bar because he never contradicted you. And his optimism was infectious. He always told everyone how wonderful they looked, and he insisted that they would find a lover that night. Eddie polished everyone's ego without asking for any reciprocation. If your face was wizened and dripping with bronzer, Eddie would tell you that your complexion was flawless. If your toupee was on backwards, Eddie would coo high praise and demand the name of your hairdresser.

The other great thing about talking to Eddie in the bars was that if you suddenly had to abandon him mid-sentence because you saw somebody cute enter the bar and you had to do some emergency cruising, he never held it against you. He was the most understanding man in New York City. And Eddie would run errands for people in the bars. He would buy them drinks. He would offer people pen and paper so they could exchange phone numbers. He would encourage the most unlikely people to go after the best looking men in the room, and some of the most surprising liaisons occurred. But never for Eddie.

Eddie did make what he thought was a wealthy friend named Dieter who needed help at his elaborate gay parties. Eddie often was assigned the task of guarding the coats at Dieter's parties, which meant sitting in a bedroom on a bed full of leather jackets, sipping a drink and trying not to spill any on the mountain of leather.

Eddie sometimes got to tend bar at an occasional party, usually late in the evening when the original cute bartender had begun to do coke or stopped making drinks early because someone at the party (sometimes Dieter himself) had taken him off to a spare bedroom. Eddie found his tasks at Dieter's parties a bit tedious, but he never lost his optimistic smile because he thought Dieter's parties would be great opportunities to meet people, which they were for everyone except Eddie. Eddie was particularly helpful during one of Dieter's parties at which twenty people OD'd. Eddie didn't leave Dieter's until he had helped the host put every single disabled guest into an ambulance. Dieter thanked Eddie for his help and showed his gratitude by giving him some coke and quaaludes.

During his first several years in New York, Eddie tried changing his look several times. He shaved his head. He grew sideburns. He let his hair grow and tied it in a ponytail. He dyed it several different colors and even tried going out at night with sequins in it. But nothing did the trick. He grew a moustache, then a goatee, and then a full beard. He tried selling himself as butch, and then femme. It was all to no avail. Every night he went home from the bars alone. Eddie had the sex life of a gay Job. But Eddie never gave up hope that he would find the right look and that his luck would change.

Eddie even toyed with becoming a drag queen for a while, but his efforts to adopt that lifestyle resulted in a severe talking-to by a delegation of the city's leading transvestites. He was told that his efforts were giving drag queens in the city a bad name, and he was asked not to buy another false eyelash or piece of lingerie ever again. Eddie hoped that he hadn't really offended anybody because that wasn't what he had been put on earth for.

No matter what Eddie did to his looks, he could never get into Studio 54. The bouncers there liked him, but not enough to let him in. They did ask him to go to the deli to get them coffee and sandwiches. In appreciation, the bouncers let Eddie stand in line with the beautiful people, but that was it. They were afraid that they would be fired on the spot if they ever let Eddie inside. One night he gave an attractive young man a camera to take pictures of the inside for him, but the young man left through another exit with the camera, and the interior of Studio 54 was left to Eddie's imagination.

Although Eddie spent a great deal of time looking for companions on the beach at Fire Island, no one ever asked him to stay over, and he certainly didn't have enough money to rent a house from what he earned spinning records at the bowling alley. Some citizens of Cherry

Grove thought that Eddie must be a celebrity's butler or gardener, because he was out there so often. But never overnight. He was the ultimate day tripper. He went out there so often that the conductors on the Long Island Railroad knew his name and Eddie knew the names of their children and grandchildren. When Eddie had a week off during the summer, he commuted back and forth from Manhattan to Fire Island every day. On the train ride out there, he would sometimes pretend to be reading publications like *The New York Review of Books* so that he would look more interesting.

One day on the train, Eddie was looking through a sophisticated cooking magazine when he saw a story about a rich bachelor who lived in a huge beach house where he cooked colorful gourmet meals for his friends. There was a photo of the bachelor sitting on the beach in a skimpy bathing suit with another very striking man. The bachelor was handing his friend a luscious looking piece of bruschetta. Eddie just knew in his heart that these two men were more than friends. As the train neared its final destination, Eddie began repeating to himself, "I will eat bruschetta on the beach with a lover, I will eat bruschetta on the beach with a lover." Right then and there it became his permanent mantra, something he said over and over to himself whenever he needed to give himself encouragement.

Eddie was out at Fire Island the day in 1981 that the panic first hit. It was a very hot Saturday in July, and the copy of the *New York Times* that was being handed around the beach in the Grove was a virtual cure for a hangover. It left many a gay man who had a deep tan suddenly looking ghostly white. A new, strange disease had suddenly broken out in some gay men who lived in New York City. Scientists did not know what was causing it, but the first ones to succumb were people who lived a rather fast-track life and had many sexual partners, two things that Eddie had been trying to do unsuccessfully ever since he arrived in New York.

As the article made the rounds, Eddie saw a couple of very disturbed men pack up their belongings and leave the beach. He never saw them again. In the weeks and months that followed, there were many such suspicious disappearances from the best looking section of the Fire Island Beach. Several houses were almost immediately put up for sale. One prominent Cherry Grove man suddenly married a woman who had been his maid. Eddie thought it would have been a great time to buy a house if he'd had any money. One of the reasons that Eddie wished he owned a house, besides not having to commute, was that he noticed that everyone who owned a house on the Island seemed to have a lover or two. Eddie often played the lottery in hopes of winning enough money to buy a house with a pool that would earn him a lover.

While the epidemic—which only grew from that moment on—terrified everyone else in the gay world, it only increased Eddie's hopes. The way he saw it, men who were extremely good looking, the ones who had been very successful in attracting partners, were now seen as major liability. It seemed to Eddie that his salad days might be coming soon. It was a great time to be ugly. Eddie thought he would be feted by men looking for pristine partners all over town. He was a gay vestal virgin, kept pure by destiny in order for love to find him during one of the darkest moments in the twentieth century. Eddie still went out enthusiastically to the bars throughout the epidemic, because he never gave up hope that someone needy would show up. He sipped his drink alone in bars, and whenever he thought his spirit was about to go south, he chanted to himself, "I will eat bruschetta on the beach with a lover." But once again, Eddie's hopes were not rewarded. The plague had made people needy, but not that needy.

At the very least, the epidemic did result in

handsome gay men being kinder to Eddie. As the death toll rose in the gay community, more and more people accepted Eddie's overtures for friendship. Especially men who were not well. They loved having Eddie around because his optimistic smile helped calm their worst fears. Eddie grocery shopped for them and was a good cook—even though it puzzled them that he seemed to serve bruschetta with every meal, even in the dead of winter. Plus Eddie always said kind and encouraging things. He told men they had never looked better, even when they were covered with lesions from the illness. He told them they were robust, even when they were barely skin and bones. He told guys on their deathbeds that they would live forever. Eddie was convincing because he had a good heart and he truly hoped that they would.

Upon request, Eddie moved in with the sick, cooked for them, and did their laundry. He got on the phone and tracked down old lovers and the families of the dying. The ailing men that he helped always tried to show their gratitude by giving Eddie the recreational drugs they didn't have the energy or time to take anymore. Eddie often went home at night to his own apartment with bags of marijuana, cocaine, barbiturates, amphetamines, PCP, ethyl chloride, and even poppers. It was the first time in his life that he felt that maybe people truly liked him. Eddie often told the sick men that they were being too generous, but they all insisted that he take the drugs. There were whispers in the gay world that these drugs were dangerous, but Eddie wasn't worried. The AIDS counselors all over town said to be careful using drugs because one might forget to wear a condom and have unsafe sex under their influence. Since Eddie, to his regret, was never having sex when he was taking drugs, that wasn't a problem. The sex that Eddie had while taking drugs was the safest and loneliest in the world. Usually, when Eddie was at home alone taking the drugs his sick friends gave him, he was chanting his mantra, "I will eat bruschetta on the beach with a lover."

Eddie probably attended more funerals in the 1980s than the Vice President of the United States. Gay men tended to be nicer and more conversant at funerals than they were at bars, so Eddie thought that the chances of striking up a relationship while mourning might not be so terrible. He always tried to sit near the surviving gay companion of the deceased because that's where most of the attention was directed at funerals. Sometimes it was hard for Eddie to choose between going to a bar or a service.

As the epidemic and the lugubrious Eighties dragged on, Eddie began taking more and more of the drugs he was rewarded with for all the errands he ran, the funerals he accompanied people to, and all the encouragement he gave. At night, alone in his apartment, he would get high and dream of all the men who had never loved him. His dreams were replete with druggy versions of bruschetta, beaches, and men. One night in the waning weeks of the decade, after he had snorted some especially potent cocaine with a chaser of poppers, he sat down at his kitchen table with a calculator. After some very peculiar computations that only Eddie himself could explain, he figured that since he had arrived in New York, he had been rejected by 1.2 million men.

The next morning, Eddie couldn't breathe. Eddie called some of the ailing people he had been helping, but all of them were too busy or too ill to come and assist him. Some of them made him promise that he would go over to their places to cook for them when he recovered his ability to breathe. Eddie finally found enough energy to dress and drag himself down to the street where he could barely lift his arm to hail a cab. He asked the driver to take him to the nearest emergency room. When he arrived at the hospital he collapsed at the front door and when he woke up he was in a bed and on a respirator.

Eddie couldn't believe how many doctors and nurses were standing around his bed. He had never seen so many human beings this interested in him in his entire life.

One of the first people to speak to Eddie was a social worker. After gathering some personal information from Eddie, she told him that she would inform his employer at the bowling alley about his illness. She also said that she had been assigned to Eddie for the purpose of giving him AIDS counseling. When Eddie told her that he didn't need an AIDS counselor because he knew enough people with AIDS, a doctor standing next to the bed gently took Eddie's hand and told him that he had AIDS. When Eddie told the doctor that it was impossible that he had AIDS because he had never slept with anyone, everyone in the room began to laugh. They sounded like the studio audience watching a sitcom. Eddie began to realize that there were dozens of people jammed into the room. There were virologists, cardiologists, radiologists, epidemiologists, psychologists, urologists, immunologists, and just about every kind of nurse and orderly. It was a very strange sight. Eddie had never seen so many professional people this concerned about him, ever. In a strange way it made him very happy, even though he felt ill in just about every part of his body. Luckily, he was out of earshot when an insensitive orderly in the back of the room said, "That's about the ugliest piece of gay ass I've ever seen in my entire life."

When Eddie insisted again to the social worker that he couldn't have AIDS because he had never slept with anyone, the social worker gently told him that was something everyone said at first, but that they would work on his acceptance issues together, that there were all kinds of new therapies for gay men in denial.

"But you don't understand, I've wanted to sleep with somebody, with everybody, ever since I came to New York, but nobody would sleep with me! I can't have AIDS.

I wouldn't even care if I had gotten it, but nobody would sleep with me. Nobody would love me. No matter how hard I tried, I couldn't get it!"

"But darling, you do have AIDS. You have no immune system and you're gay," said a sweet and comforting voice at the foot of his bed. For a minute he thought it was his grandmother, but it was a doctor.

Eddie kept insisting that nobody would sleep with him. He tried to shout out the utter truth of his loneliness so everyone in the room would hear him, but it was to no avail.

"Darling, we don't care how you got it. We're going to take good care of you. We're going to give you the newest experimental treatments."

"But I don't have AIDS!"

The laughter in the room was making him confused and lightheaded. He started crying.

"Now, there, there. We're gonna work on this together," said the social worker. I'm gonna help you understand what's going on. Doctor, don't we have something that can help make Eddie sleep?"

One of the nurses plunged a needle in his arm, and as Eddie began to fade into unconsciousness, he could hear that the people in the room were still laughing.

When Eddie awoke the doctor was the only one in the room. she had the kindest smile he had ever seen. He really wished that she was his mother or his grandmother. The doctor told Eddie not to worry, that they were giving him the latest drugs for AIDS, some that had bypassed animal testing and come directly from the laboratory. Best of all, He wouldn't have to pay for them because the federal government was paying for everything that needed to be done for AIDS patients.

"But I don't have AIDS."

"Eddie, where did you go to medical school?" the doctor responded, somewhat snippily. Then she tried to lighten things up. "I bet you have a big fancy medical degree and you're hiding it right there under that pillow, aren't you?"

"How can you have AIDS without sex or a lover?" asked Eddie.

The doctor smiled like a bemused parent and said, "Eddie, you have sex-negative, lover-negative AIDS!"

"Did you give me a test for the virus?"

"We didn't need to. We could tell from your immune system and your symptoms that you have AIDS. We don't want to waste our health insurance premiums on unnecessary tests, now, do we, darling?"

"But I never had sex. I never had love," Eddie moaned.

"The social worker is coming in a little while. She'll help you through this. Remember Eddie, we love you. You're very important to us. You're a very special patient."

Eddie couldn't believe it. For the first time in his life he was being told by important people that he mattered.

When the social worker appeared, she brought a large thick pencil with a pad of paper and asked Eddie to draw a picture of two men in bed. Eddie was extremely weak and had trouble lifting his hand to draw, but he made an effort. All he drew for her was a single stick man in a stick bed.

"That's wonderful. We'll keep working on it. We'll draw every day, until you can put another man in that bed. And then you'll tell me the name of that man, and every other man who was ever in bed with you. And then I'll give them a phone call and pay them a visit and say that a very thoughtful man from their past just wanted me to contact them and tell them that he's very, very sick."

She came back every day for a week, and every day Eddie just drew the single man in bed alone.

"Try a little harder to draw another man in bed. I know we can make a breakthrough," the social worker said.

It might have continued that way indefinitely except for the fact that Eddie was growing so weak from the treatments they were giving him that one night he began to have hallucinations. The following morning when the social worker gave him the pad, from somewhere inside him he miraculously found the energy to draw for a few hours while the social worker sat in shock.

What Eddie was drawing was no mere sketch of a stick man in a lonely stick bed. Even though it was only done in pencil, it was a fully realized illustration that almost looked like a classic oil painting—the details and gradations of dark and light were so subtle and profound. The drawing looked like it was coming from the hands of Andrew Wyeth or Thomas Eakins, rather than Eddie. He completely ignored the social worker's request to draw two men in bed, and instead had drawn two exquisite men in the nude on a beach. In the distance over a magnificently rendered dark churning sea, he had drawn a sun with a vaguely human, optimistic, smiling face. It gave the portrait an otherworldly, almost mythological effect. The two princely beings were lying on a blanket, and the miraculous precision of Eddie's sketch was so good that the social worker said, "My God, he's feeding his friend bruschetta, right? Eddie, what is the meaning of the bruschetta? And Eddie, what are the names of the two men? Where do they live? Did you sleep with both of them? What kind of sex did you have with them? Were you on the top or the bottom? Did you use a condom? Do you remember their phone numbers?"

The effort had completely wiped Eddie out and he fell back on his pillow and lost consciousness.

The social worker ran three floors down to Eddie's doctor with the drawing. The doctor was just as astounded as the social worker. "Do you think it is what I think it is?" asked the social worker.

"Absolutely," said the doctor. "It's a near-death art

experience. It won't be long. I'd better call the administration."

In Eddie's final hours, he was surrounded by dozens of doctors and nurses who all watched in awe. Virtually everyone who worked in the hospital came by to see Eddie. And it wasn't just inside the hospital that attention was being paid. Outside on the street a huge throng of reporters was gathering. There were also representatives of every AIDS organization in the world, even some from as far away as Africa. There were balloons and cannons loaded with confetti. Eddie was wheeled over to a window so he could see the crowds of well-wishers. Some had placards that said "Happy One Millionth!" Eddie's vision was going and he couldn't quite make them out. He was however, able to speak for the first time in many days. In a faltering but determined voice he asked, "Who are these people? Why are they here? Do they love me?"

The doctor, who had attended many seminars on ethics and terminal illness, had a strict code about talking to the dying; she believed in always telling patients the truth.

She leaned over and said, "Darling, you are the millionth person to be dying of AIDS. You're going to be on the front page of every newspaper in the world. You are a very special person to all of us. You're very famous and you've never looked more beautiful. We do love you."

Thank God we only hear what we want to hear, because all that Eddie consciously took in at the end was that he was special and was loved. The last human sounds that penetrated his consciousness were the huge rounds of applause that came from the doctors and the cheers from the street. It was very difficult for anyone to hear in the room, but those closest to him could make out the one final word that emanated from Eddie: "Bruschetta."

Daddy's Little Clown

The father was not doing the greatest job of hiding his disappointment. The mother looked at him in horror as she stood behind their son who had just told them that he'd decided he wanted to be an attorney.

The father mumbled something about supporting his son, no matter what he did in life. The son should be the best of whatever he wanted to be. Money would be no object. The father's voice was so low and tentative that the son wasn't sure whether or not he had really meant that he was proud. The mother nervously jumped in and started hugging the son and telling him that this was one of the greatest days of her life, while the father excused himself in a whisper and went into the bathroom.

The father selected the largest, fluffiest white bath towel and buried his face in it so that he could muffle his sobs. He was disgusted with himself, but he just couldn't control his emotions. As he tried to drown his face in the towel, a second round began. It wasn't crying, it was deep, almost funereal weeping. This was his first born, the one in whom he had invested his keenest hopes. He still had four other sons who could make his dreams come true, but the oldest one is always a prince in his father's eyes. His eldest, a golden law school-bound lad, would have brought feelings of complete masculine fulfillment to just about any father in the land. But this stunning eldest son had not given his father his fondest wish: that his first born become a clown.

The mother urged the son to phone the grandparents with the news and then she headed to the bathroom. She knocked on the door and told the father to meet her in their bedroom. He had barely closed the bedroom door when he collapsed in his wife's arms, and together they fell into a heap on their bed.

She begged him to be strong.

"I won't let you down," she said. "I haven't failed you yet."

"It's not your fault."

"I've given you four other wonderful sons. One of them is bound to be a clown."

"Do you really think so?" he whimpered.

"I know so."

She really didn't know any such thing, but she was desperate. She couldn't stand it when men who have hair growing on their backs started to cry.

"We'll take them to more circuses," she said soothingly.

"But they've already seen them all."

"Well, we'll just do it all again until they get the point."

For years the family had been coordinating its holidays and vacations with circuses all over the country. With their balloons and funny hats, they caused general mirth on every airplane that they spread out in. The slightly disheveled, mischievous little family could often be seen waiting with autograph books at the performers' entrance to circus tents. Each of the boys always wore an elastic bound ball-like nose, sometimes under protest. The little red noses often had a runny little human nose beneath them. At an early age, the boys were thrilled with the family outings to circuses, but eventually most of them sensed that there was something terribly odd about their family.

It all started in the early Cold War, when the father, then a young recruit, had been assigned to bodyguard a four-star general in Paris. The general was supposed to figure out how to protect the Eiffel Tower in case of a nuclear attack by the Soviet Union. During his free time, the young soldier explored the cultural treasures of the City of Lights. One spectacular spring day, he stumbled upon a little French circus on the outskirts of Paris, and after the confusion of finding the right currency for the ticket, he went and sat down inside the musty tent. Before he knew it, his entire future had been transformed.

As the father sat in the audience with a croissant and a glass of red wine, the planets conspired to bring him together with Annie Fratellini, inarguably France's leading clown, and from the perspective of connoisseurs, the greatest clown in history. Annie Fratellini was the archetype of a clown.

The father had come from a poor family that didn't even have enough money to introduce its children to the joys of the circus. He had never even seen one on television because his family didn't own one. The father was a Big Top neophyte, and Annie Fratellini was his first live clown.

When Annie Fratellini waddled out to the main ring of the circus in her big shoes and floppy hat, it might as well have been Venus herself. Every light inside the father went on. Her big sensuous painted smile and her eyes darkened like black moons from another world simultaneously brought laughter and tears to the audience. For a man who had never slept with a woman, her wildly feminine, hilarious performance was equal parts spirituality and sexuality. She was cosmic. He was having what only can be called a spontaneous mythopoetic awakening complete with all the psychosexual trimmings.

Each one of her routines, drawn from the long history of clowning, was a sublime revelation to the father. When she juggled, it was as though she was tossing stars in the air. When she sang, it was like hearing all the rivers of the world sing to him. And he didn't even understand what she was singing, though in his soul he imagined that she was singing about the unfolding of his own life. Her act defied logic and chronology. One moment she seemed to be a young, rambunctious clown, and the next she was a loopy, arthritic, ancient clown. Her sleight of hand took his breath away as she made the largest bouquets of beautiful flowers disappear into her body.

He didn't know how she did it, but she was able to play several instruments at once, a virtual one-woman band. She seemed to play the saxophone by bending all the way back and coming out from under her own legs. Annie Fratellini was showing him all the amazing things that a creative woman can do with her body. He was totally aroused. Every time she did a pratfall, he longed to be on the ground beneath her to prevent injury. But she was invulnerable and indestructible. For the father, the image of Annie Fratellini altered for the rest of his life his deepest desire to merge with a woman: love and sex would henceforth be intimately intertwined with the vision of the great clown, Annie Fratellini.

Back in his room at NATO headquarters that night, Annie Fratellini continued performing in his imagination. While other men in his unit might fantasize about their scantily-clad pin-ups, the father conjured up all the incredible things he could do in bed with a clown.

The father went back to the circus as many times as he could before he was transferred back to the states, and when he left Paris he didn't care that he was leaving the Louvre and the Seine behind. The only treasure he would miss was Annie Fratellini. The stewardesses on the plane commented to each other about the lovesick soldier who stared at a photo of a clown throughout the flight.

Shortly after he returned to the states, to Dubuque, he left the service and tried to decide what to do with the rest of his life. He thought about finding a fully-accredited clown school, but he was honest with himself and had to admit that he did not waddle or wiggle like a clown. He just didn't have it. His body movements were more like those of an accountant, which is what he became. Instead of becoming a clown himself, he would sire one. He would marry and have a daughter. And he and his wife would give the child the kind of zany upbringing that was necessary to nurture a great clown like Annie Fratellini. But before he had a daughter who could become a clown, he needed to find a good woman to marry.

Fortunately, Dubuque had caught on to the Mexican food craze early, and one evening the father was chowing down on a burrito when he noticed the woman who would become his beloved. She was sitting with her secretarial pool sisters in a margarita-and-nacho celebration of one of the women's five-pound weight loss.

It was the Fifties, and in those days people were not aware that margaritas are more of a drug than a drink. The restaurant had what is called a bathtub margarita, a nearly bottomless bathtub of the aforementioned drink with twenty- and thirty-foot straws extending from tables all over the restaurant. Nearly every diner was having the bathtub margarita, including the father and his soon-to-be wife. When the future wife went into the bathroom, she was so tanked she could barely locate her face in the mirror as she freshened her make-up. She was so out of it that she even got lipstick on the wall of the ladies room. Well, of course this cosmetic disaster made her look like you-know-who.

When she emerged and the father saw the wild colors and unprecedented designs on her face, he was so overcome by flashbacks to Annie Fratellini that he was a goner. Years later neither could recall what was said, only that they met and somehow managed to give each other correct phone numbers, despite the fact that the margaritas had begun to make everyone in the restaurant sound like they were speaking a foreign language.

When they dated sober, she looked more like Mamie Eisenhower than Annie Fratellini, but in those days, in many Midwestern towns, Mamie was what passed for hot. After numerous dates, they decided that their feelings for each other were just as strong when they weren't drunk as when they were, so they decided to marry. And this

49

happened despite warnings from her family about men who took a woman on too many dates at the circus.

The mother tried to be supportive of her husband-to-be's obsession with clowns and the Big Top. She thought that it was better to have a man who has jolliness in him than not. They were married inside a huge tent and the bridesmaids were a little chagrined to have to wear bowlers and taffeta with polka dots. The event struck many of the guests as being more like a big children's birthday party than a wedding.

Their married life revolved around the father's successful accounting career. And his dream. He wanted a large family to increase his chances that one of his daughters would grow up to take the circus by storm. This is where the first hitch occurred, because, try as she did, the mother could not give birth to a girl. In rapid biological succession, they had five healthy sons and then the couple stopped trying because they were worried about how they would be able to send the ones they already had to clown school. The paucity of daughters came as an existential shock to the father, but the mother kept insisting that men make fine clowns too.

Privately, she thought that she was unable to give birth to a girl because she had been painfully jealous ever since he told her about Annie Fratellini. What women's magazine tells us how to compete physically or emotionally with a clown in a husband's past? When they made love, she could never be sure whether he was really making love to her or to his French icon. There were nights when she felt like there was a goosey Parisian clown lying there in bed between the two of them. But to get through this life, every woman makes her choices and her trade-offs.

The father struggled to give his sons the kind of childhood that any professional circus performer would envy. The house was painted all the bright primary colors used by Ringling Brothers, and they filled their children's playrooms with oversized balls and whoopie cushions. They even bought an expensive battery-operated car into which, on cue, all five sons would cram themselves dressed in their little clown costumes. Whenever their neighbors were having a backyard barbecue, the family was always invited. All seven of them arrived at the parties in full formal clown costumes, which amused everyone to no end. Their reputation as the weirdest family on their block was unchallenged.

The parents thought they had given their progeny an entertainment-packed childhood complete with the solid building blocks of audience participation, charm, and aggressive buffoonery that would lead to a successful adult life of a clown. They were not at all prepared for their oldest son's announcement in his senior year of high school that he was hanging up his carnation with the hidden water jet in order to enter college and law school.

And the bad news did not stop there. The second son wanted to become a politician. And the darkness continued to fall upon the family when the third son told them he planned to enter medical school. The father was beginning to understand that life has a propensity to break your heart. He looked a tad crazed when his fourth son took his parents aside and told them that his career path would not take him into the realm of the greatest performers, but rather into the three rings of the great thinkers; he would become a philosopher.

The fourth son's announcement was qualitatively different from the others. There was an edge to it, a very negative one. The father sensed an anger beneath his son's career decision, as though it was meant as a complex punishment for his parents. But as with the other sons, they put up a good front, and the mother rushed out to Carvel's to purchase a big ice cream clown cake to celebrate the announcement. It turned out to be one of the most ambivalent evenings the family ever spent together.

The father was on the money about the fourth son, for he truly dove into philosophy with a vengeance—against his family. And as is the case with any angry academic, someone gets hurt in the process. This time it was Hannah Arendt. The fourth son put the banality of evil in his crosshairs and decided to spend the rest of his life proving the clownishness of evil. Evil was hardly banal—not in the least. It was as clownish as the day was long. And clownishness was the root of evil, its very essence.

He quickly made a name for himself in the narrow and controversial field of philosophy called Evil Theory. Only the biggest universities have endowed chairs devoted to the exploration of the nature of evil, and at a very young age he was given one at an Ivy League school. He published dozens of groundbreaking papers on the clownishness of the Inquisition, the clownishness of witch-burning, the clownishness of slavery, the clownishness of the Holocaust, and even the clownishness of capital punishment. Perhaps his most talked-about work was a paper trying to show the connection between clowns and the crucifixion of Christ. More than one fellow philosopher quipped that he probably had Hannah Arendt perpetually spinning in her grave.

The fourth son always made a point of sending his articles, which were invariably published in prestigious philosophy journals, home to his parents, who sadly read each word out loud, even the hard to understand ones on "the reification of the clownishness of evil." They didn't fully understand the papers, but the father usually caught the drift and he would sigh deeply and say to the mother, "He hates us, he really hates us."

Predictably, the fifth son provided the *coup de grâce* with a twist. After making sure that his parents were sitting down, he informed them that his plan for the future was to become "a gay."

"A gay?" his father shouted.

The mother immediately dreaded the years ahead. But in all fairness, the parents made every attempt to be cool about the orientation announcement. And there was at least one fringe benefit: Becoming "a gay" did not entail the expense of going to college. All that was required was moving to New York City.

The father was crestfallen, and given his advancing years, the mother desperately tried to convince him that there was not that much difference between being gay and being a clown.

"Stop humoring me," the father said. "They're worlds apart. They're apples and oranges. There's not even a remote connection. Gays are boring. You're libeling clowns."

"Listen to me. I raised that boy. There are things he just can't hide from his mother. I've watched him like a hawk. One day he is going to make you proud. Deep down inside, that boy is a clown."

Their fifth son moved out of the house and made his way to Manhattan where he became a bartender, a waiter, and then wrote a novel about coming out in the Midwest. Meanwhile, from the moment he left home, his parents kept reviewing the details of his youth trying to figure out what they could have done better.

Early in childhood, when he wasn't wearing his clown costume, their fifth son often donned women's clothes, and it hadn't escaped their attention that he looked good in them. Remembering how Annie Fratellini had rapidly crossed back and forth over the gender lines in the blink of an eye, the father had high hopes that his son was developing a repertoire that would come in handy years later in some prominent North American circus. It was not easy explaining to their neighbors that the tiny drag queen was preparing for a major career in show business. They even let the son bowl publicly at the local alley in the mother's high heels. He also had free reign at his mother's make-up table. Unfortunately, with his keen eye and sure hand, when he was done he often looked more like a ten-year-old Joan Crawford than a budding Annie Fratellini. It galled the father that after being so supportive of the son's adventures in flamboyance, it had only resulted in him becoming a gay.

A number of years went by during which the parents received letters from the fifth son about boyfriends, bars, and brunches, but little that would pass for confirmation of the mother's so-called intuition. The father started to think that she made the whole thing up so that he would not lose interest in life. When they received the son's coming out novel, he was certain that there was no hope, for the book was so tedious that neither of them could read more than half of it.

But then a miracle happened.

It was after the ten o'clock news one evening several years later when they were flipping around on the television set and they saw a familiar face bobbing up and down like a marionette on one of the talk shows. By God, it was their fifth son, the gay.

He was shouting at the talk show host, "IT'S A PLAGUE! YOU'RE ALL MURDERERS! WE'RE ALL GONNA DIE!"

Just when the talk show host got him quieted down, he started screaming again, "THE GOVERNMENT'S NEGLIGENCE IS KILLING US! THE GOVERNMENT'S NEGLIGENCE IS KILLING US!"

The performance astounded his parents as much as the people on the talk show. Their son's face turned every angry shade of red and his eyes were popping in and out of their sockets, as if they were fake eyes. And his hair, which was now receding, had become a vigorous orange fringe that gave him a very contemporary Clarabelle look.

The effect of the son's uncontrollable shouting and

wild over-the-top body movements struck his parents as utterly hilarious. They both fell on the floor, howling.

"I can't believe it. Maybe he hasn't let us down. I hope the camera shows us his feet. I bet he's wearing big floppies."

Then the son began to attack his own people, the gays. "YOU'RE ALL RESPONSIBLE FOR THIS EPIDEMIC! YOU'RE ALL GONNA DIE!"

To further dramatize his point, he stood up for a second and then sat down with such force that his chair collapsed backwards.

Well, it's a good thing that the mother was wearing Depends, because both parents lost it.

"He's doing the Crazed Napoleon routine!" the mother shrieked.

"I know, I know, and bless him, he's doing it perfectly!" gasped the father.

As the talk show ended, the son screamed into the camera, "IT'S AN EMERGENCY! IT'S A CRISIS! NO MORE BUSINESS AS USUAL! THE PRESIDENT MUST DECLARE A NATIONAL EMERGENCY!"

The father traveled back in time and saw his little Emmett Kelly sitting on his lap begging him to tell him again about Annie Fratellini's Crazed Napoleon routine. It was his father's favorite. When all three rings of the French circus were filled with the action of nearly every performer in the circus, Annie Fratellini would suddenly appear in the midst of them all dressed as Napoleon, complete with her hand tucked inside her little jacket, which was covered with all kinds of impressive looking clown insignias and epaulets.

In her oversized Napoleon hat, she began screaming out orders at every one in the circus. They weren't even really words. They were just screeching, vaguely hysterical sounds. Even though the noise made no sense it seemed to overpower every single performer in the circus, including all of the animals. A dark, sinister, almost erotic trance of human execration and abjection seemed to seize every soul in the audience, including the father. The audience roared with the loudest, most other worldly laughter that the father had ever heard. One by one, everyone in the circus tent seemed to fall into servile obeisance. Everything had gone completely out of their control. At Annie Fratellini's feet were the trapeze artists, the dog trainers, the dogs, the dancing bear trainers, the dancing bears, the lions, the lion tamers, the zebras, the French poodles, the human cannonball, the other clowns, and even the ringmaster himself. Then for a second, the entire audience paused in absolute silence so all that could be heard was the piercing sound of Napoleon Fratellini's comic will to power. The audience seemed to levitate in total delirium. Before them stood not a clown but a superhuman genius. The fifth son loved the story, and sometimes his father would catch him trying to act it out. When he was alone in his room he would often shout all kinds of orders at his toys and then have a frustrated tantrum when they did not obey his orders.

Life had taken a strange turn for his son. The plague had given him a stage on which to fully realize his talents.

Unfortunately, the son's appearance on the talk show was also taking the mother back in time and the faultline beneath herself and the father was turning into a virtual earthquake.

"See," she said, "why did you doubt me? Can you forget her now? Who cares about her? I feel cursed by her. Look at our son. He makes her look like Soupy Sales. Don't you see? I haven't failed you. I've given birth to the biggest clown of the twentieth century. Damn Annie Fratellini. Damn her! Damn her! Damn her!"

The father was so excited about the son finding himself that he didn't pay much attention to the mother's outburst.

In the weeks, months, and years ahead the fifth son was a constant presence on network news hours and talk shows. Whenever their son was on television, they made a real occasion of it. They blew up balloons and threw confetti at each other. They ate Jujubes and popped corn. They would even have calliope music playing in the background while, on one prime time show after another, their son was screaming, "END THE PLAGUE OR REVOLUTION! END THE PLAGUE OR REVO-LUTION!"

Although the father was elated at the son's fame, he began to withdraw into himself and wonder exactly what the legacy of Annie Fratellini had done to his son. As he watched his fifth son become the leading clown of the plague by constantly doing the Crazed Napoleon routine, the father remembered him dressing up in drag as a child, and he grimly suspected that his son was literally trying to become Annie Fratellini to please his parents. His son was trying to transcend time and gender to become her. He had never told his son that he wanted him to become her, but the father was convinced that his son had tried to become the fulfillment of his father's obsession. It gave the father chills.

The son's performances became more and more elaborate. He turned screaming at talk show hosts into an art form. Like Annie, their son seemed to be attempting to control every element of the plague with sheer loud will. Activists, doctors, nurses, even elected officials were like his elephants and French poodles. They all bowed to his ear-shattering, overpowering looniness. If he told them to go left, they went left. If he told them to go right, they went right. There was no rhyme or reason to what he told them to do. It was pure unpredictable, irrational entertainment. And no one was immune. Even the President of the United States seemed to be listening to their gay son screaming out all kinds of final solutions for AIDS and doing whatever he said to do about the plague.

One night on a *Nightline* telecast while he was urging Americans (in an explosive menacing voice) to bring the government to its knees in order to end the plague, the parents watched as their son crossed and uncrossed his eyes while touching his nose with his tongue. They had never seen anything like it. They hadn't laughed so hard in years. It added extra years to their lives.

The country was so taken by their son's performances that at times the government's policies concerning the plague began to resemble the Crazed Napoleon act. Their youngest son, the gay, had the entire United States in the palm of his hand and totally at his command. Government officials who were handling the plague got so rattled by his veiled and not-so-veiled threats that they felt they had no choice but to supply all the sick people in the land with any and all of the medicine that the son demanded in his routines on television. An endless round of experimental drugs was given to the sick at the shrill behest of their son.

The son was clearly impressed by his own angry performances, because he himself eventually took every single one of the medications that he had demanded the government offer, and inevitably they took their toll on him and destroyed his immune system. Soon the ghost of Annie Fratellini could no longer be seen doing the Crazed Napoleon routine on television and one day the inevitable phone call came to the father and mother.

"Father, I am dying. May I come home?"

"Of course, son. You've made us proud. We love you. Come home."

When the fifth son arrived home, he was a pale shadow of the ballistic man they used to see on talk shows. When he walked into his childhood home, the reunion was overwhelmingly emotional. The parents put him in his old bedroom which now had walls covered with pictures of the family visiting circuses all over the world in happier days.

The other four sons were called and told that the youngest did not have much time. They dutifully journeyed home from all over the United States. They all spent the last day of the fifth son's life surrounding his bed, trying to express their love and unity with him by all wearing their red clown noses. Across America, the plague was bringing families together exactly like this. Some people argued that reunions like this one were what made the plague a good thing, that it was a kind of morning in America. For a brief moment, the parents were happy to be with all of their sons again in one place, even if the occasion was a sad goodbye. They were now all grown men, but for a second the father felt as though all his sons were cramming once again into that little car for one big comic effect just to make their old man happy. It was heartbreaking to see the mother, the father, the lawyer, the doctor, the politician, and the philosopher, all in clown noses, gathered around the bed watching the gay brother die.

There was one very unpleasant moment near the end when the philosopher son and the father seemed to be exchanging hostile glances over their red noses. (The philosopher son hadn't wanted to wear the nose, but given the gravity of the situation, he acceded.) The philosopher son seemed to be saying to the father that the plague itself had been caused by clownishness, and in response the father's eyes seemed to say the opposite, that the plague would be ended by clowns.

The youngest son was buried, after a surprisingly somber and quiet funeral, in a clown costume. When the four sons returned to their homes and families, they felt a relief that lasted the rest of their days.

The Coma

When Gregor finally awoke from his coma, there was only one nurse in the room and her name was Candace.

There were literally thousands of coma specialists who wanted to be in that room, along with countless scholars of the Holocaust, but the team of experts who had been following Gregor's coma—some for decades—thought it best if only one person communicate with him. Candace was chosen to be the attending nurse partly because she had some psychological training. She probably was picked mostly because she was a lesbian, but that wasn't discussed openly.

A number of doctors had suspected that Gregor was bilingual because, even in his coma, occasionally he could be heard mumbling both English and German words. The doctors had also selected Candace because she had majored in German before she left college to attend nursing school.

Candace couldn't believe he was a man in his late seventies because Gregor still looked like he was in his early twenties. His facial coloring was still ruddy. He looked like he was a sleeping Ralph Lauren model.

The doctors all agreed that it was the strangest coma they had ever seen. There hadn't been one quite like it in all of recorded medical history. Gregor was lucky that one of the guards chose to hit his head exactly where he did before the concentration camp had been liberated. Ever since scientists had tried to determine how Gregor's traumatic brain injury caused both a coma and a virtual state of suspended animation so that he didn't age a day in fifty-three years. Gregor was living proof that one could launch human beings into a state of suspended animation if one could traumatize the brain in just the right manner. Mankind could learn a great deal from Gregor's long, mysterious survival. It might even lay the basis for biological time travel.

For over a decade, coma researchers had been trying all kinds of new drugs and surgical techniques, and the field of coma therapy had expanded exponentially. There was the expectation in the field that comas would soon be as easy to treat as bacterial infections. Gregor had recently been given a radical new form of magnetic stimulation of his cerebral cortex, as well as a new drug called anti-melatonin, and the scientists had become very excited when they began to see dramatic changes in his MRI scans. Word had begun circulating in the neurological community throughout the world that the gay concentration camp survivor might soon come out of his fifty-three-year-old coma.

Holocaust scholars were soon doing cartwheels and gay politicos were elbowing each other out of the way to be the first to meet him.

Candace had been asked to begin spending long hours closely observing Gregor because the coma recovery experts didn't want Gregor to panic when he came out of it. They wanted someone comforting, one of his own people, to be at his side. They expected him to have one hell of a headache.

Candace had been training for a year on how to ease Gregor psychologically from being a gay man in a concentration camp in 1944 to being a gay man in 1997 in New York City. Candace had been reading as much as she could about Nazi Germany and the gay lifestyle in the concentration camps so that she could easily bond with Gregor when he came to.

Candace was on the phone talking to her girlfriend Della the day that Gregor started to stir. She put the phone down when she heard Gregor try to say something.

Then miraculously, he began to make sense.

"Horst? Horst? Horst?" were the first words that Gregor said.

"Horst is not here right now," said Candace who was hoping that he really did know English so that she would not have to use her rusty German.

"Where am I? Is this London?" asked Gregor.

"No, Gregor. You're in America."

"Where is Horst?"

"He's not here now." Candace did not know who Horst was, but she had a troubling intuition about who he might be. She decided to be vague about some things because she didn't want to give him the kind of shock that might bring about a relapse of the coma.

"Hitler, where is Hitler?" asked Horst.

She thought it would be helpful to give him the good news. "He's dead."

"Who killed him? The Russians?"

"No, he killed himself."

Gregor started to cry. Candace gently touched his hand.

"Am I dreaming that Hitler is dead?" he asked.

"No, you're awake. You've been asleep for a long time."

"How long?" he asked.

"Fifty-three years."

"I don't believe you," he said.

"Yes, it's strange," she said. "But it's true."

"Where are the guards?"

"There are no guards here."

"Where are the guards?"

"They are all dead."

"Who killed them?"

"The Americans."

"Where is Horst? Is Horst here?"

"No."

"I want Horst."

It was many days before Candace could break it to him that Horst was dead. He said he knew it in his heart, but he didn't want to believe it. He wept the tears of someone who has held them back for half a century.

The doctors thought it would be months before Gregor could get out of bed, so it was Candace's responsibility to sit and talk to him, read to him and try to give him a sense of what he had missed for the last five decades.

Gregor was amazed at the things that Candace told him. She showed him all the modern devices that had been invented since he had been beaten into a coma. She showed him VCRs and microwaves and cell phones and personal computers. Orderlies wheeled a big television set into his room and they let him watch it for an hour a day while Candace tried to explain current events to Gregor.

Candace encouraged Gregor to talk about Horst in order to work through the grief. Gregor was totally bereft. It was as if Horst had just been murdered.

Gregor explained that they had been lovers for a year before they had both been taken away to the camp.

Gregor told Candace that Horst could see what was happening in Germany, that he hadn't been fooled. Horst had warned his friends about what was coming, but no one believed him.

Gregor and his friends, one by one, began to disappear from Berlin. Their families made up stories. Some said their sons were studying overseas.

Horst had a sneering, sardonic way of talking to Gregor about the disappearances. He would say, "It's a matter of public health. The Fuhrer is trying to rid the country of an infection. Soon the blood of the nation will be clean."

Horst would refer to Hitler sarcastically as "Herr Doctor."

As Candace listened to Gregor, she was glad that the doctors in the hospital had kept their distance.

Gregor told her that when their closest friend,

Wilhelm, was taken away, Horst notified Gregor by saying, cryptically, "Wilhelm is undergoing therapy. He is infected with a virus that threatens the German people. They will render him non-infectious."

Gregor told Candace that when he asked Horst if they were on Hitler's list of infected people, Horst told him, "Herr Doctor has everyone on a list."

Gregor was stunned as Candace recounted the progress that gay people had made all over the world. She told him about Stonewall, Bette Midler, the Castro, leather hot pants, and The March on Washington. She even tried to explain lesbian feminism to him.

"It all sounds like one of the Fuhrer's tricks," said Gregor.

"What do you mean?"

"He always liked to make people think they were going one place, when in reality, they were going to another."

"Hitler's really dead, Gregor. Everything's changed. It's a new world for gay people. Just look at me and Della."

Candace's lover Della had been artificially inseminated but there had been a slight mix-up and she was about to give birth to quintuplets.

"This is America!" she said. "Lesbians can even have five babies at once, if they want to."

Gregor nodded, but he looked introspective, as if his mind were really still in the old world.

As Gregor was adapting to his new circumstances, unbeknownst to him, an enormous political battle was being waged.

Every gay organization in America was clamoring to get Gregor as a spokesman as soon as he left the hospital.

Needless to say, the most vocal and demanding of all were the AIDS organizations. For years many of the AIDS activists had compared the AIDS epidemic to the

Holocaust. Now they had the opportunity to recruit someone who had really been there and done that.

The activists threatened to cover the hospital with a giant lubricated condom if their demands were not met, so their demands were met.

The AIDS activists were the first outsiders allowed to meet with Gregor. They wanted to prepare this very important post-comatose gay citizen for the AIDS Millennium. They insisted that the first gay people that he would encounter in fifty-three years should be fully-accredited AIDS educators.

They were concerned that Gregor had been in a coma during the formative years of the gay movement. They were very concerned that some gay activists from the liberation era would get to Gregor before they did. They were eager to recruit Gregor to do public service announcements, in which he would look into the camera and say, "AIDS is a holocaust, I ought to know."

Candace was not happy about the AIDS activists meeting with Gregor. He had only recently been able to sit up in bed. He continually talked about Horst, and from what he told her, she had a feeling that these activists might not be the best people for Gregor's health. But the hospital administrators were afraid of the commotion the activists might make if their demands were refused, so they insisted.

When the activists first entered Gregor's room, all of them were wearing black T-shirts with angry slogans. Their fists were in the air. Gregor began to tremble. Candace had to reassure Gregor that they would not hurt him. She reminded him that they were Americans in the 1990s, not Germans in the 1930s.

As soon as they were all in the room, they began to chant, "WE'RE HERE, WE'RE QUEER, AND WE'RE NOT GOING SHOPPING! WE'RE HERE WE'RE QUEER, AND WE'RE NOT GOING SHOPPING!"

The AIDS activists had a wild look in their eyes and

the whole scene felt vaguely familiar to Gregor.

One of the AIDS activists immediately gave Gregor the universal AIDS orientation lecture. The basic point of the talk was that everyone would die if they didn't do what the AIDS activists told them to do.

Gregor was quite shaken. And then it happened: All of a sudden a golden cloud materialized before Gregor's eyes and he could see Horst standing at the foot of his bed looking imploringly at him. Horst looked as tall and handsome and wonderful as ever.

Gregor motioned to Candace to come over to the side of the bed and then he whispered into her ear, "Horst is here now. Please, take these people away."

Candace turned to the AIDS militants and said, "I'm sorry, but Gregor is suddenly feeling very sick. You'll have to leave now."

"We'll be back tomorrow," said one of the activists. "AIDS is a crisis. Everyone must get involved. Even people who have been in comas. People who have been in comas who don't fight AIDS are murderers! Anyone who isn't dead must join in our crusade!"

As soon as the activists left the room, Horst was no longer there.

Candace had to give Gregor a sedative to calm him down.

The entire coma treatment staff was very apprehensive that Gregor might have a relapse.

But they were even more concerned about the activists who threatened to stand outside the hospital singing AIDS folk songs until they were allowed to see Gregor again. Most of the top administrators had heard AIDS folk songs. They were very, very afraid.

Gregor begged Candace not to let the activists back in, but when she explained how the activists had threatened the welfare of the entire hospital, Gregor had a flashback to a time in his life when he heard stories about what happened to all the patients in some hospitals in Germany. He didn't want to be responsible for anyone getting hurt. He sadly acceded to Candace's request.

When the activists marched into Gregor's room the second time, they were in an even more aggressive mood.

They were accompanied by a woman who was the leading AIDS folksinger. She carried a large guitar and her hair was festooned with red ribbons. One of the activists proudly told Gregor that the woman was the Joan Baez of AIDS, which didn't mean much to Gregor.

The woman immediately began strumming her guitar and she started singing songs about the triumphs and tribulations of AIDS activists. The song celebrating the fact that now every single government committee on AIDS contained AIDS activists was catchy but seemed to go on forever.

Then she sang an up-tempo song celebrating the HIV test. Everyone joined hands and sang the chorus which was simple but very affecting: "AZT should be free, AZT should be free, AZT should be free."

The activists urged Gregor to sing along, but he really didn't seem to understand the words, because it sounded like they were singing "Zyklon B should be free, Zyklon B should be free."

When they were done singing, the most important AIDS activist in the group made a speech to Gregor. He told Gregor that as a gay man who had survived the Holocaust, he had a moral obligation to help them end the AIDS Holocaust. "If you don't help us, you're a murderer!" the man screamed at him.

The activists told Gregor that he had become an international role model for young gays, and they wanted him to go on television and urge gay people all over the world to stop hiding from their doctors and to go and be tested for the virus that the government had declared the official cause of AIDS. And Gregor should urge them, if they tested positive, to allow the government to treat them with all the new experimental treatments. And if they were not positive, they should all volunteer for vaccine experiments.

Every time they used the word "experiment," Gregor began to shake.

They told Gregor they wanted him to go to the White House to meet the President and be the first person to take the new AIDS vaccine.

Gregor turned whiter than the hospital sheets on his bed.

Suddenly, Horst was standing upon a golden cloud there in the room again. Gregor recognized a familiar look of barely contained horror on Horst's face.

Horst was saying something inaudible, but Gregor could read his lips.

"Candace, Horst says these people are kapos. He wants you to get these kapos out of here. GET THE KAPOS OUT OF HERE!"

This unnerved the activists, who looked at each other sheepishly.

Candace begged them to leave quickly.

As they shuffled out, they sang an AIDS folk song about how gay men should be medically proactive and devote their lives to AIDS activism.

When they were gone, the golden cloud and Horst disappeared again.

That night Gregor developed a terrible fever and night sweats. When Candace came in the next morning, her worst fears had materialized. He had relapsed into his coma. The doctors rushed to his room from all over the hospital. They tried all the new drugs and innovative anti-coma electronic therapies in their arsenal, but nothing seemed to work. It was perhaps the most unusual and intractable coma in history and, to this very day, they are still trying to get him out.

The Last Lovers on Earth

The phone began ringing on Monday morning and Kyle couldn't get a thing done. He was sure that it was their friend Enola who had spilled the beans to one of their neighbors who worked in the media. They had both begged her to keep it a secret. She hadn't realized the significance of their status until Seth, after one too many glasses of chardonnay, had underlined it all too well for her. She suddenly got the point that it was really big news that they were both still alive.

The first call came from the local ABC affiliate. It was a blond woman whose name Kyle recognized from the evening news. She said that she was sorry to be asking such a prying question, but was it true that Kyle and Seth were lovers, and was it also true that they were the only gay people on earth who were still alive?

"Last time I checked," he responded.

"Do you realize how amazing that is?" she asked.

"Well, I guess it is slightly unexpected."

"We'd like to lead with you tonight on the five o'clock news."

As soon as Kyle hung up the phone it rang again. It was NBC. Then CBS, CNN and several internet news services called. Then an aggressive reporter from the *New York Times*, and after that just about every major paper in the country.

And all this was happening simply because Kyle and Seth were gay and alive.

Throughout the day on ABC they promo'd the evening spot: "Tonight at eleven, we'll have an interview with the last two gay men alive on earth."

All day long hyperventilating reporters called AIDS researchers around the world and asked them to explain why these two men could possibly be alive. The phone lines at the Centers for Disease Control in Atlanta were constantly tied up. What was going on? For several years now hadn't the top AIDS researchers insisted that, as a result of the government's unprecedented multi-trillion-dollar federal effort against AIDS, all gay men were dead?

Now word of the confirmed spotting of two gay men who were still alive was spreading all over the globe.

Was there a cover-up going on? What did the government know and when did it know it?

The media was not ready for another major government scandal, especially one that involved a minority group that was supposedly history.

For the press it looked like it could become a story about criminal negligence in science. If the top scientists could not be trusted to tell the truth about AIDS, what could they be trusted to do?

But for scientists who were informed of the bizarre fact that two gay men were still alive, the question was purely scientific. Calmer heads had to prevail. The right questions needed to be asked. The correct scientific procedures needed to be agreed upon in order to get to the bottom of this new gay men's health crisis. In science, method and careful data collection are everything. What was different about the two gay men who were the only ones still alive? Did they have unique immune systems? Were they genetically different from all the other gay men? Had they forgotten to take their medications? Had they failed to understand the complexities of treatment compliance? Had someone forgotten to give the two men one of the experimental vaccines? Was this an exception that was going to prove some disturbing rule? The matter called out for well-designed experiments with proper controls to determine why all the other gay men on the planet were dead and these two were still alive.

In every editorial conference at every newspaper

across the country, the same question was being asked: How was it possible that so many amazing medical approaches to AIDS had been tried without having any effect on these two gay gentlemen? A real opportunity was at hand; there was a great deal scientists could learn by studying this unusual gay couple. They were as valuable as the last two pandas on earth. Perhaps these two men should be urged to be volunteers for one final AIDS study that might help the government understand the true nature of gay men once and for all. After all, every other member of their community had been enthusiastic team players in signing up for nearly every government protocol that had been offered to them.

When the Director of the National Institutes of Health was informed that two gay men were alive despite all of the billions of dollars that the N.I.H. itself had devoted to AIDS, he asked the President to make an exception and have the Secret Service assigned to protect these two medical anomalies. He was a worldly man and he knew that there were millions of homophobes all over the world who, as a result of the success of the AIDS research effort, had given up hope of ever having a homosexual to attack. These two gay men would be in demand everywhere there were homophobes. They had to be kept safe and alive if scientists were to achieve a final understanding of the AIDS epidemic. What had the best minds in science done wrong? The fact that these two gay men were still kicking gnawed at the conscience of every scientist at the Bethesda campus of the N.I.H.

Since all the gay men in every other country were dead, it didn't make America's AIDS researchers look too good; they always put on airs that they were the best in the business. The heads of health departments all over the globe were calling Washington and demanding an explanation. Had the arrogant, dishonest American scientists fucked up again? Everyone in the AIDS Division of the Pasteur Institute in Paris could barely keep from gloating. It was yet another reason that the entire international AIDS research effort should have been kept in French hands. There were no gay Pierres or Michels living in Paris anymore. The French AIDS research effort had been completely successful, thank you very much. The Americans could just kiss their dreams of a Nobel Prize for the eradication of AIDS goodbye.

When Seth got home, Kyle was ashen with terror.

"Why did you have to tell Enola that we were the last two gay men alive on earth?"

"I told her to keep it to herself. What a bitch!"

"Well, I hope you're ready to go on the *Larry King Show*."

"What?"

"They just called. They played hardball. They said that if we did any other media before them, they would never have us on. And they warned us that they were the only show that wouldn't give us a hard time."

"I can't go on *Larry King*. I just got a zit on my nose."

"They're sending a limo in an hour. I don't think we have any choice. I don't want to be grilled mercilessly by Barbara Walters."

"What do they expect us to say?"

'They want to know why we're gay and not dead."

"I'm just gonna sit there and smile. You'd better do all of the talking. You're the reason we're still here."

No one was more shocked than the editor of the *New York Times*. The whole building on West 43rd Street was in disarray. It was as if a car bomb had hit the place. Just the week before, the *Times* had done a five-part wrap-up series on the epidemic with the headline "All Homosexuals Dead, But AIDS Researchers Still Cautiously Optimistic." It had been an expensive and historic series to pull off; no one at the Old Gray Lady looked forward to retracting this one. They couldn't just run a little correction. How had they gotten the story so wrong when they had enlisted practically every reporter in the building to scout the entire globe to make sure that every gay man was indeed dead after such a prodigious government research effort? Had the *Times* once again failed to uncover a major government scandal? How had they not known that there were still two gay men carrying on, practically under the *Times*'s nose, in Cape May, New Jersey? Why hadn't anyone on the team of investigative reporters thought to call the Cape May Health Department to see if there were any gay men still alive in that town? This was no minor oversight. Heads of reporters were going to roll down Broadway. This would be the biggest media brouhaha since CNN's Vietnam sarin mess.

Religious groups that had breathed a sigh of relief when they thought that the AIDS epidemic was over immediately began to plan mailings warning that Seth and Kyle could be responsible for recruiting a new gay population if something was not done to counter the threat.

The staff of the *Larry King Show* was ecstatic about their coup, but Larry wanted balance and it looked like they wouldn't be able to get it. They desperately tried to contact the leading AIDS researchers to come on with the gay couple, but the scientists were so mortified that they didn't even answer their phones.

The Centers for Disease Control convened an emergency meeting of its elite Rapid Response Epidemiologic Service, which had successfully concocted the whole paradigm which the nation had come to know as AIDS. The Epidemiologic Service of course wanted to pass the buck. They insisted that it was the fault of the CDC's AIDS Prevention Department. If that department had done what it was supposed to do—namely, convince every gay man to take all kinds of AIDS drugs prophylactically, just in case they got AIDS—this crisis would never have materialized. How could anybody in Prevention call himself a professional? Nobody looked good in Atlanta. There was AIDS egg on the face of everyone at the CDC. Some doctors around the country talked openly of charging the entire organization with medical malpractice.

The Prevention Department was dumbfounded. Every time that there had been an announcement of a major breakthrough in AIDS therapy, several hundred thousand gay people had taken advantage of the new opportunities. And there had been so many of these remarkable medical breakthroughs that it was inconceivable to the Prevention Dept. that any gay men could still be standing. How could it be that Kyle and Seth were walking around without the famous buffalo humps, which had been the fringe benefit of protease inhibitors? Why hadn't they developed the chicken feet, ostrich plumes, and lion manes that were the side effects of the subsequent generations of breakthrough AIDS pharmaceuticals? Clearly the marketing departments of the leading AIDS pharmaceutical companies had fallen down on the job. Someone had seriously failed in the area of AIDS communications.

"It's the Vaccine Education Department!" said one nervous high-level CDC official to the angry director.

"You mean these two gays never took the vaccine?" responded the director.

"No, sir."

"What's the matter with them? Don't they own a television set?"

That two gay men had actually survived the massive Manhattan AIDS Project, the most ambitious biomedical enterprise in history, led the news hours all over the world that night. Some stations interrupted their regular program to break the story about Kyle and Seth. People in many countries had forgotten what a gay man looked like, so ambitious photographers from dozens of countries were booking flights to the small airport in Cape May. Many media outlets had to scurry to find experts on homosexuality to go on the air to give the public adequate background for the unfolding story.

It was only a few hours after the call from the local station when, Kyle and Seth's street suddenly started to fill up with camera crews and curious neighbors.

When Kyle looked out the window, he yelled at Seth, "See what you've done for us? There goes our peaceful little life in Cape May!"

"Well, it's your fault. You told me not to believe a word that the government said about AIDS."

"For God's sake, you'd be dead if you had, silly."

"Kyle, I don't want to be an international celebrity. I just want to go to the A&P. We're out of coffee."

They embraced anxiously and tried to collect themselves. When the limousine from Larry King arrived and they emerged out their front door, some neighbors actually applauded, but there were some who took the opportunity to dust off some vintage homophobic epithets.

"Go back to Israel, you gay Jews!" one rather confused and angry person in the crowd shouted at them.

"We're not even Jewish!" screamed Kyle as they darted into the waiting limousine.

Helicopters with cameramen leaning out of them could soon be seen and heard buzzing loudly overhead. The limo's progress was followed all the way to D.C. It was turning into a media event not seen since the O.J. Bronco chase or the Cunanan hunt back in the 90s. All three network anchors of the news were called in early to cover the story. Swat teams of reporters had located Seth and Kyle's parents and were now beginning vigils outside of their parents' homes. Never had two gay men caused so much commotion merely by not being dead.

The President of the United States was interrupted in the middle of a National Security Council meeting and informed that the Central Intelligence Agency, the Federal

Bureau of Investigation, and The Bureau of Tobacco and Firearms had all confirmed that the news reports were accurate. It defied logic, but yes, two gay men were still alive. And even more surprisingly, one of the wire services was reporting that they were as healthy as football players.

The President turned red and started pounding the table. "Get me the CDC on the phone in the Oval Office," he shouted at his secretary. He promptly ended the meeting and rushed out of the room.

The director of the Centers for Disease Control was nervously waiting on the other end of the phone when the President took his place behind his desk. The President took a deep breath.

The director immediately started to pass the buck. He tried to blame the Secretary of Education. The two undead gay men had not received sufficient AIDS awareness education. And it was Hollywood's fault for not doing enough AIDS-awareness movies. In addition, it was decadent Broadway's fault for never having enough red ribbons on the Tony Award shows.

The President was not having any, and he proceeded to lose it on the phone. He ordered the CDC to determine immediately what was wrong with their AIDS program. He demanded a report on his desk in two weeks. How did they know there weren't other gays all over the country who hadn't been beneficiaries of the government's generous AIDS treatment and vaccine program? Privately, the President was thinking that this was the kind of thing that always happened when you let the government bureaucracy run things. He had always told his staff that they would have been better off privatizing the whole damn AIDS crisis.

As the limo sped with its precious cargo to Washington, the major networks recorded the entire journey from the air. They did a split screen showing Republican leaders rushing to the floor of Congress to denounce the resurgence of a powerful homosexual lobby in the Nation's Capital, even though Kyle and Seth had never been there before. They blamed the democrats for an incompetent AIDS program. Fundraisers in Christian right-wing offices watched the limo with the gay couple on television and began composing letters in their heads that warned of the threat of a new homosexual agenda in Washington.

There was a television set in the speeding limousine and Kyle and Seth watched their own journey in horror. Kyle took advantage of the car's wet bar to make the two of them a stiff drink.

"This is so surreal," he said to Seth.

"It's like the first days of the epidemic."

As Seth sipped his drink and stared out at the passing scenery, his eyes teared up and he got lost in memories of the preceding twenty-five years. He remembered the two of them being paralyzed by the news every night as the death toll kept climbing and climbing while the government declared one major victory after another against AIDS. Every time there was some new development in AIDS therapy, it seemed to Kyle and Seth that another herd of gay people disappeared. All of their friends had become alienated from them. No one understood why they didn't show up at AIDS benefits. At gay parties in Cape May, whenever Kyle said that they didn't believe what the government or Gay Men's Health Crisis were saying about the epidemic, they were told that they were paranoid or in deep denial. They were not criticized in this manner anymore because, as a result of the program that all their gay friends supported, all of their gay friends were now dead. They had all wanted the government to take extraordinary measures to end the epidemic. And it had.

When they arrived at the CNN building, the limo pulled into an underground garage to avoid the crowds of cameras outside. Seth wanted Kyle to beg the driver to take them back to Cape May immediately.

They were greeted as soon as they got out of their car by one of the *Larry King Show*'s producers. She told them that the whole world was waiting to see them, that virtually every news show in the world had called in and asked for a live feed from the broadcast. Larry King himself was so excited that his cardiologist was called in to sit on the set during the interview. The producer told them not to worry, that Larry never hurt anybody's feelings during interviews. He would treat them just like they were family. He would ask a couple of phony hardball questions and that would be it. She also said that they wouldn't let any nasty calls get through. She said she realized how rough it was for them.

"We want to protect you," she said. "You two are like an endangered species."

"Like?" said Seth. "We are an endangered species."

After spending two hours in a plush refreshment suite at the studio, they were taken into the Green Room on the King set. They were told that they would not meet Larry until they were on the show because he liked things to seem spontaneous and unrehearsed.

Larry King started the show by apologizing for bumping the Publishers Clearing House winner who was supposed to be on that night.

"I know the whole world is talking about this story," he said. "Tonight we have the exclusive. Even though the United States spent a quarter of a century and an unprecedented amount of money on AIDS research, treatment, and prevention, there are still two gay men alive. It's almost unbelievable, but we have them here on the show for you tonight.

Larry handled the frightened last gay couple on earth with kid gloves. They both warmed up to him right away. He acted fatherly in his concern about their sudden international notoriety.

"You both know that you've caused quite a stir all over the world, don't you?"

"Yes, Mr. King," responded Kyle.

"Call me Larry, please."

"Yes, Larry. All hell has broken loose."

"What's it like being the last gay couple on earth? It must feel like quite a responsibility."

"Nobody knew it till one of our friends was indiscreet. But now the whole world knows. I guess we have to try and do a good job representing the gay community," responded Kyle.

"Especially since I guess we are the gay community," added Seth.

"We understand the White House has issued a statement assuring the American public that it is re-examining its whole AIDS program in light of this development," said King. "They're baffled over at 1600 Pennsylvania Avenue. They just can't understand how after spending over two trillion dollars on the AIDS problem, the two of you could possibly be sitting here chatting with me tonight."

"Well, here we are, Larry," said Seth nervously.

"So the two of you just never got with the AIDS program. You know I was kind of surprised not to see you both wearing red ribbons. I remember in the old days of the AIDS epidemic, you just never saw a gay without a red ribbon."

"We never wore red ribbons, Larry," said Kyle.

"That's interesting. How many AIDS candlelight vigils did you two attend?"

"None, Larry."

"And how many dead bodies of people who died of AIDS did you throw over the fence onto the White House lawn in demands for more money to be spent on the AIDS Manhattan Project?"

"None, Larry, none."

"You know, I'll be criticized by everyone in the media if I don't ask this, and I hope you take it the right way. Are you two sure you are gay?"

"Of course, Larry," asserted Kyle.

"I mean you have to admit that in half a day you not only have attracted the attention of the whole world, but you've shaken our faith in the American scientific establishment. You understand why I have to ask these tough questions."

During the call-in segment of the show there were all kinds of curious questions. Some people wanted to know whether a single gay couple actually constitutes a legitimate minority group. Another wanted to know whether Seth and Kyle qualified for the benefits of the Americans with Disabilities Act. One woman who described herself as a lonely fag hag asked if she could adopt the couple. Kyle told the woman that they had enough women friends, including one with a big mouth.

The most dramatic call was from the head of the Secret Service who called Larry to say that the President had authorized around-the-clock protection for Seth and Kyle, because they were now extremely important to the public health of America and until all the leading AIDS researchers understood fully why Kyle and Seth were still alive, the AIDS Manhattan Project could not be considered a complete success.

Larry sat up in his chair and said, "What do you think of that, Kyle? Complete protection from the Secret Service, just like the President."

"Well, that's good, I guess," he said with a gulp.

Larry closed the evening by thanking the couple for sharing their amazing story with the American people. He said that he would love to have them back on the show periodically for as long as they were still alive.

Because Kyle and Seth were so important to the

security of the country, the Secret Service never let them return to their home in Cape May. Instead, they were flown to a retired C.I.A. safe house enclave in Palm Beach, Florida. Needless to say, the Service knows that we are a country of crazies, and as soon as anyone hears that there are only two of anything left in existence, there are always a few Americans who feel a deep need to shoot them.

Kyle and Seth actually found living in Palm Beach wearing fright wigs and dark glasses to be quite pleasant. They were housed in plush places reserved for ex-spies and mafia rat finks. The government provided for their every need, with the understanding that they would cooperate in helping the top AIDS researchers understand why the AIDS Manhattan Project had failed. They didn't get to see their families, but that wasn't bad because their families now felt embarrassed and guilty that they were related to the only two gay men still living on earth, two men who had also brought shame upon the world's greatest scientists.

They were interviewed daily by brigades of psychologists, sociologists, theologists, and AIDS educators. Not since the O-ring brought down the *Challenger* had there been such an intense American effort to get to the bottom of what had gone wrong with a government endeavor. Why had every other gay person taken the treatments or the vaccine except for Kyle and Seth? What was different about them? The government had spent a fortune on public service spots to get the cooperation of all gay people. Why had Seth and Kyle not been motivated to follow the public service urgings of celebrities like Madonna, Whoopi Goldberg, or the incredibly influential Rosie Perez? The government needed to have a firmer understanding of its communication failure for future public health emergencies.

The experts just wouldn't accept the rather simple answer that Kyle gave them. He said that starting when he was a teenager, and continuing into his adult years, he had come to the conclusion that the American government didn't like gay people all that much. In addition, it seemed to him that we primarily expect our government to lie to us and screw everything up. He pointed out that if you accept these basic premises, you would pretty much do what he and Seth had done, which is steer clear of anything that the government was doing on AIDS. They had better things to spend their time on. And incidentally, they wanted to live.

Not a single AIDS expert who examined the lovers could believe that it was that simple. They were attractive, intelligent men. While they did lack some of the perky desire to please that the scientists had noted in many of the dead gays, they seemed reasonable. Why had they not responded to the carefully crafted, powerful, and sexy ads that the government had used to motivate gay men to get tested and to take the vaccines and pharmaceuticals that had been especially prepared for them? There had been AIDS ads of hunky guys with great abs climbing mountains, AIDS ads showing hot guys rolling in the grass with their dogs, ads with rapturous transvestites donning condoms, even multicultural ads with pictures of gorgeous black guys on bicycles next to copy that said they were using their freedom of choice to select which AIDS medication they wanted to take. These ads had worked for every other gay person on earth except Kyle and Seth. One exasperated AIDS educator suggested that the reason that Kyle and Seth hadn't cooperated with the AIDS program was that they were sexually dysfunctional. They were not responsive to the erotic subliminal messages that Madison Avenue had perfected for the government to utilize throughout the war on AIDS.

"Actually, we like sex," Kyle told the psychologists.

"You've seen one AIDS ad, you've seen them all," said Seth.

After a year of vigorous research on the matter, the government didn't know any more than it knew when the two were first discovered living in Cape May.

Every week that passed after the discovery of the lovers was filled with a great deal of anxiety for the White House. The President was running behind in the polls for re-election, and his opposition was constantly running pictures of Seth and Kyle, accusing the administration of total failure on AIDS. The President himself made a direct appeal to Kyle and Seth to take the AIDS vaccine. He even offered to have it administered to them at the White House during a special ceremony with Sharon Stone attending, but they respectfully declined.

On the night before the election, the President called the directors of both the Centers for Disease Control and the National Institutes of Health to tell them that they had probably cost him his re-election. "You both told me you would end the AIDS epidemic. You've really let me and the country down."

When the results came in, all the pundits said the President had lost because of Seth and Kyle.

In his concession speech at a Washington hotel, the President tearfully admitted that his failure to end the AIDS epidemic completely was the reason for his poor showing at the polls. He said that he had done everything that the AIDS activists had demanded that he do, but apparently that was not enough to end the scourge once and for all. When he said that he hoped that the new President would put politics aside and commit himself to whatever public health policies were required to put the epidemic finally behind them, the crowd of his supporters roared their approval.

Among the millions of TV viewers watching the President concede the election were Seth and Kyle, who were sitting side by side on a big sofa at their secret location. They didn't know exactly what the defeated President meant by his remarks about public health, but once again in the course of the epidemic, they found themselves putting their arms around each other and holding on for dear life.

Banned in Boston

I should have seen what the future held for me when I took a high school career aptitude test and it suggested that I could excel in the field of food preparation. I didn't let that keep me from my dream of becoming a gay writer; I come from a long line of bullheaded men and women who never take no for an answer.

But the indications that I had chosen a disastrous career path came as early as the first gay and lesbian creative writing course I signed up for shortly after I had graduated from college.

It was the early Eighties and I was in my peachy gay youth. I signed up for a popular writing class taught by a gay novelist who had sold more than three thousand copies of his first five novels.

By the third class, it was pretty obvious that I didn't fit in. After we read our first stories aloud, we were supposed to comment honestly on our colleagues' stories, but we were never told how honest we should be. I crossed the line when I told one of my classmates that his coming out story was so poorly written that he should have stayed in the closet until he learned the English language. He immediately started crying and two lesbians rushed to his side and I spent the rest of my first creative writing course in the gay and lesbian doghouse.

Since it was the beginning of you-know-what in the Eighties, the theme of most of the stories by the men in the class was safe sex, if that can truly be called a theme. (There were some in that class who thought that being cute in a bar was a theme.) It was amazing how many of the safe-sex themed stories ended with a line like, "And then reader, I put on a condom, a really big one."

In the later Eighties I took another creative writing

course from a gay novelist who was also a professional safe sex instructor. He always seemed to have a banana hanging out of his backpack.

He and I didn't get along too well because he thought that all gay men's fiction should be filled with what he referred to as "fessin' up." He was known as the father of gay literary "fessin' up." There was so much fessin' up in that class that I thought we were in the interrogation room at the sixth precinct.

And what exactly did he want fessed up in our writing? You got it. He wanted gay men to fess up to the fact that they were responsible for the AIDS epidemic. He called for brave existential fessin' up in our gay short stories. He urged each one of us to become the Dickens or Tolstoy of fessin' up. He didn't care whether it was a boy-meets-boy, boy-buys-condom, boy-gets-home-on-Fire-Island, or a coming-out story. There was no fessin' up in my stories, so I was warned that I would never get published by the gay and literary establishment because he said that nearly every publishing house in New York has a fessin' up quota requirement for its submissions. It was fascinating to see even lesbians writing stories with gay male characters fessin' up all over the place. To tell the truth, lesbians fess up gay male characters even better than gay men do.

There was so little about AIDS in my stories that the instructor thought I was taking the course by mistake.

"Are you sure you're even queer?" he asked in exasperation.

"No, I'm not a queer," I responded.

"Then why did you take this queer writing course?"

"It was supposed to be a gay and lesbian writing course," I said.

"Same thing," he said.

As he said this, I imagined my instructor coming out to his parents: "Mother and father, I have something wonderful to tell you. I'm a big goosey queer." I could see the celebration going on for days.

There were tears of frustration in his eyes near the end of the course when he gave us his final evaluation of our work by saying to the class, "I've done my darnedest to turn you all into multi-cultural queer writers, and all I get are these crossover assimilationist pieces of crap! What gay and lesbian gratitude this is! One after another of you has written a white, gender-specific short story without a mass AIDS die-off. No red ribbons! No candlelight vigils! No fessin' up! This is an atrocity. What is going to happen to queer literature? I fear for our gay and lesbian bookstores. They'll all go out of business. And what the hell are people going to read in the queer studies courses in the next millennium?"

I thought, how about Shakespeare's sonnets? Maybe a little Whitman or Proust?

He looked at me and screamed, "And you, what do you have to say for yourself, Mr. Porter?"

"I guess I wasn't born to fess up or celebrate gender diversity. I didn't know we were going to be writing propaganda for multi-cultural queer AIDS activism."

"Mr. Porter, I knew what to expect from you when you turned in your first story. None of your characters exchanged a single clean needle."

"Well, sir, none of my characters was a junkie."

"That's a terrible thing to call someone who is chemically dependent. Especially a queer."

"Well, none of my characters was a queer chemical dependent."

"That's not an excuse. I think you're AIDSphobic, Mr. Porter. I think that gay literature is going in one direction and you're going in another. If my intuition is correct, I detect that you are trying to write crossover gay literature. The queer market is queer, Mr. Porter. It will never cross over. You're trying to pass, aren't you, Mr.

Porter? As a result your work will never be accepted. Your work will never make it into the bibliography of a queer studies program, not even one at a retarded community college."

"Well, I was just hoping enough gay people would read my stories that I could make some kind of living at it."

"I wouldn't quit my day job, Mr. Porter. The other problem I have with your work is that it doesn't cross-dress enough. Mr. Porter, have you ever worn a dress?"

"Not since Halloween in the Seventies."

"That's what I thought."

"A gay short story that does not cross-dress is not a gay short story. It's a straight-acting short story."

In the last story I wrote, I had included a cameo of a Third World transvestite character in a hot air balloon. But it was too little too late.

I soldiered on through one gay creative writing course after another for many years. You name the gay writing program and I was there. Harvard. Yale. Yaddo. The New School. Bimini. But somehow I just never fit in anywhere.

It was at the New School that I penned a rather nifty—if I do say so myself—story about a blind gay man who comes out at a nudist colony. It was not easy to write, especially the action scenes. I was devastated when I was told that coming-out stories were now old hat, that I was a decade behind the gay times.

The only time anyone showed even remote interest in my work was when I took a gay mystery writing course from the leading lesbian feminist mystery writer. She opened the class by saying that she was a stickler for craft and insisted that there are only six basic gay and lesbian mystery plots and all of them involve lesbian murders on English chicken farms.

I showed great discipline. Virtually every story I wrote involved a lesbian getting iced on an English chicken farm. I usually located my chicken farm near London and I threw in a ton of fog for atmosphere. In my stories I shot lesbians, I stabbed lesbians, I ran over lesbians with cars, but always on an English chicken farm. It was only when I thought I was being a little creative and shifted a lesbian murder to a German health spa that I was politely asked to leave the class.

All the money I spent learning how to write ultimately did little for my career. Everything I sent to gay literary magazines seemed to come back with a rejection letter. I was constantly told that my writing was too assimilationist. One editor even called me an "Auntie Tom." It looked like nothing I ever wrote was going to appear in a gay or lesbian publication. At bookstores like A Different Light and Lambda Rising, I would never be more than a customer.

A life of flipping veggie burgers flashed before my eyes if I didn't get with the program. As a last ditch attempt I started attending every annual Gay and Lesbian Writers Conference. Which was a big mistake.

At the first one I attended, a novelist who had written a 2000-page novel called *Queer Like Me*, gave the keynote address in which he attacked the gay community for not buying enough of his books.

I was booed heavily during the question and answer period when I went up to the microphone and asked him why, if he wanted people to buy his books, he didn't write something they wanted to read. Someone in the back of the room began to scream "queerphobe" at me, so I sheepishly returned to my chair and didn't ask another impertinent question for the rest of the conference.

I noticed that the same people are at every one of these annual conferences. And they all noticed me, too. I quickly became a marked man. All the gay literary editors put me on a little list. I could see the rejection slips piling up for the rest of my days. No witty little gay and lesbian literary cocktail parties for moi. I was writing old fashioned gay stories and the world wanted multicultural queer literature. I was a throwback.

And then the final blow came at last year's Gay and Lesbian Writers Conference, which was held in Boston.

There were a total of 1,200 writers at the conference. Since that is the average sale of a gay and lesbian novel, I think we know the audience for whom our writers are writing.

All the literary supergays were at the conference. These are the people who decide who will get published and who will spend the rest of their lives cursing the lavender muses for not blessing them. And these are the people who banished me once and for all from gay literature.

What did I do?

Oh it was awful, just awful.

I should have known better when I arrived at the conference. The place was swarming with literary and cultural law enforcement. The gender police were there, as well as the multi-cultural police, the bisexual police, the condom police, the AIDS activist police, and even the turkey-baster police. There were so many literary and cultural arrests prior to the first plenary session of the conference that everyone was a bit edgy. I got a very dirty look from someone sitting behind me when I whispered to the person next to me that I thought there was so much policing going on in gay arts and letters that I wondered how anyone had any time to do any writing.

The keynote address was given by the man universally regarded as our most important gay novelist because there are over ten thousand deaths from the complications of AIDS—all of them his nearest and dearest friends—in his novels. His most recent novel looked like a gay Arlington National Cemetery. In his presence we all felt inadequate. Some of us neophytes had yet even to start a body count in our fiction.

He opened his talk by announcing the deaths of a few more gay friends and then launched into AIDS fire and brimstone like I have never heard before. He was interrupted by applause so often you would have thought that Oscar Wilde had come back from the grave. He went into high fessin' up. The audience exploded in cheers when he said that our behavior had resulted in the biggest plague of all time. And when his eyes rolled back in his head and he said that unless we nominated him for the Nobel Prize we were all going to die, the crowd was on its feet, applauding wildly.

It did not go unnoticed that everyone in the hall was standing and screaming hallelujahs except me.

When they finally calmed down, the novelist wound up his inspired talk by calling for a leftist queer AIDS revolution in America: "And in closing, I want you all to remember that none of us will be free until every transgender queer in Pocatello, Idaho, who wants a free sex-change operation gets one!"

At that point, something urgent and naughty and self-destructive in my soul made me stand up and shout, "Well then, Mary, we ain't never gonna be free!"

That was it. They came at me from all sides. Every officer from every imaginable division of the gay and lesbian cultural police. And a good thing too. The audience was about to take the matter into their own lesbigay hands.

I was shackled and not only taken out of the conference, but Boston proper too. I was blindfolded, thrown into a car and the next thing I knew I was walking around Worcester, Massachusetts.

Banished forever from queer literature, I decided to taunt destiny no longer. I signed up for the next available class at a culinary institute.

Now whenever I pass a gay bookstore and see a shiny new queer multicultural AIDS epic in the window, I think sadly of what could have been.

The Kimono Party

As Everett and Shea were getting dressed, they watched a gay news show on cable television. The program had very inexpensive production values and occasionally the picture froze on a frame with the lesbian news anchor's mouth wide open in a state of paralysis, like a reaction shot from a dice-and-slice movie. The image was perfect for the kinds of stories she was reading, mostly from gay newspapers published all over the country.

The anchors had just shown a film clip of one of the country's right-wing religious leaders saying the all-too-familiar line about gay folks, that he hated the sin, but loved the sinner.

Two of the sinners were presently trying to pick out appropriate ties to wear to the party as the right-winger debated the self-declared gay leader. As he stared at the TV screen, Everett's brow became deeply wrinkled. He didn't quite know where to begin. Everett was not too fond of the so-called gay leaders who stood between him and God-only-knows-what. He was famous in his dwindling circle of friends for dropping lines like, "How many gay leaders does it take to screw in a light bulb?"

As Everett listened to the mushy gay spokesperson debate the bloodthirsty right-winger, his face reddened. "They're gonna get us all killed," he said. "Someone should check these guys for a pulse."

When they cut back to the man and woman who were anchoring the gay news, the woman read a story about a man with AIDS in prison in Florida who, over a three-day period, had been beaten to death by prison guards. The man had barely survived the initial assaults and was placed in the prison hospital, but the guards eventually found their way to his room and finished him off in the hospital bed.

Shea winced at the television and then looked out the window. With a forlorn sigh he said, "Do we really have to go to this thing?"

"No, but let's at least try," said Everett.

Neither one of them seemed to be in a party mood, so Shea had made them martinis to sip while they dressed and watched the rest of the gay news.

The two anchors of the gay news had a peculiar way of mugging a dirty look at the camera after every story to show their displeasure with what they had just read. Everett had never seen anything quite like it before. The woman read an item about a man who had come out to someone in a small southern town. When word spread to some of the man's neighbors, they had then broken into his house and attacked him with baseball bats. When his mother tried to call the police, they pulled the phone out of the wall and beat her up, too, until the gay man reached for a machete under a bed and scared them off. As the lesbian anchor finished the story she scowled into the camera and the other anchor rolled his eyes.

"Brokaw and Jennings better watch out," said Shea.

It was getting a little close in the room, so Everett put on the air conditioner. It was awfully warm outside for an autumn evening.

"If I had to read news like that every week, I'd probably make faces, too," said Everett.

"I guess that we're lucky we can even see news like this at all," replied Shea. There was a note of world weary sarcasm in Shea's voice. A shivery feeling of failure spent a moment in Everett's consciousness.

Everett always wanted to throw himself in front of oncoming reality where Shea was concerned. Not only did Everett feel helpless, but there were times when he thought he made things even worse. Where the epidemic was concerned, Shea had become the lover who knew too much.

Everett and Shea were always very late for parties, and this was no exception. Not even the fact that they really hadn't been invited anywhere for a long time seemed to matter. Across town the guests were already arriving. Some showed up fully dressed while others donned their outfits in the host's bedroom. It was one of the first gay kimono parties anyone had thrown in years. Some gay historians insist that Mae West held the first one and that J. Edgar Hoover may have thrown one or two, but nobody was really sure.

When the first arrivals asked the host who else was coming, the host nervously spilled the beans that Everett and Shea would be among the guests. That did not go over very well. One of the early guests looked curtly at the host and said, "Oh, it's going to be one of those kind of evenings. I didn't know that those two were even still alive. What a waste of good kimonos."

The host didn't have the heart to tell them that Everett and Shea would be the only ones there without kimonos. The host tried to fix things up by saying, "Oh, Everett's promised he won't say anything to rain on anyone's parade."

"I feel so sorry for Shea," said one of the younger guests.

An older guest contradicted him. "Don't pity Shea. He's become as bad as Everett. He eggs him on."

"Should we take off our red ribbons?" asked a tall man in a black silk kimono that was appointed with a single red ribbon, the universal symbol of AIDS awareness.

"Don't be silly," said the host. "You have the right to wear your red ribbons. They haven't made Everett the gay Fuhrer yet."

That said, a couple of the guests nonetheless removed the red ribbons from their kimonos. One said, "I'm sorry. I hate scenes. I failed confrontation in high school."

"Suit yourself," said the host.

"Give me your ribbons. I'll wear several. I'm sick of Everett's bullshit," said a man in a white silk kimono.

"They just can't handle the truth," said the host.

"They just haven't met the right AIDS educator," said the man who now had several red ribbons on his white kimono.

The host was getting very anxious about Everett and Shea arriving without kimonos. Everett was adamant, so the host reluctantly gave him permission, as long as they wore expensive business suits. "You two will be rich Western businessmen, and we'll all be gold-digging geisha girls," he had said.

Everett and Shea were now dressed in their very best suits, but they were not making any moves to leave the apartment. They were going to be even later than usual. They were watching the last segment of the gay news, the part where the male anchor named all the celebrities that he thought were gay. This was the part of the show that always made Everett say to Shea, "Something has gone terribly, terribly wrong with the gay world."

"I can't believe he just announced that all those people are gay," said Shea.

"He should work for the National Enquirer," replied Everett.

"We'd better get going."

"What if I make us one more drink? Just a small one."

"Don't make it too small."

Everett really didn't want to go. He knew most of the people at the party hated him. The great network of AIDS activist high society would be there. All the gay muckety-mucks. He wasn't happy about the reason he thought that they'd been invited. The host had been chilly for years, but Everett's appointment as the Director of the

Hannah Arendt Studies Department at the New School had impressed him. There had even been an article about Everett in the *Times*. He was now a minor celebrity. The appointment had caused indignation in gay venues all over town. The *Times* had coronated him as a promising New York intellectual. He knew that until then most of the people coming to the party had written him off. This turn of events had made them all nervous. Somebody they had exiled from the gay zeitgeist was making it.

His status was not the only thing that was changing. He knew that the gay zeitgeist's confidence in the government was beginning to be challenged by events. Gay leaders all over the city were beginning to worry that something weird was going on and that the AIDS dissidents were right. Over the years, Everett had loved causing trouble by supporting the dissidents at gay parties. Whenever the subject of AIDS came up and someone mentioned the small group of scientists and journalists who thought the government had gotten everything wrong about the epidemic, or was covering up the truth, Everett had always spoken up for the dissidents.

"Didn't you all used to be dissidents?" he would ask his former friends. "Didn't you used to be a persecuted minority group before you became masters of the AIDS universe?"

They would look at him dismissively. For the most part they would never openly contradict him. They took him out of their rolodexes; they didn't invite him to Fire Island or the Hamptons. He and Shea became the butt of private jokes.

Occasionally, one would work up enough courage to lob a petulant line or two at Everett: "Do you think there's a conspiracy, Everett? Is the government out to get you and Shea?"

Everett just didn't know what to do with gay men. He couldn't live with or without them.

As he handed Everett a drink, Shea once again asked, "Are you sure you want to go?"

"We have to. We're winning. We have to show those assholes we're not afraid of them. It's all changing, and they know it. Maybe not consciously, but deep down they're all scared out of their dim little wits."

"Well, if you change your mind, I still have those two steaks and we still have all those shiitake mushrooms your mother gave us."

Most of the people were now into their second drink at the gay kimono party. The novelty of the kimonos had now become secondary to the fact that Everett and Shea were coming. An evening of gay fantasy was threatened by the impending arrival of an unpleasant man who'd made everyone in a kimono at the party tense for years.

"So Miss Hannah Arendt and her dog Toto will soon be here," said one of the outraged gay men in a kimono. "May I hit him up for some money for my AIDS Testing Foundation?" asked a man in a bright pink kimono.

"Didn't he once call you an AIDS kapo?" asked a man in a blue kimono.

"He compared us all to kapos. He said we're all collaborators," said the man in the pink kimono.

"Whenever he opens his mouth, I feel like I'm doing a scene from Casablanca," said the man in the blue kimono.

"It's more like Shoah," said the man in the pink kimono.

"I'm not butch enough to be a kapo," said the man in the blue kimono.

"What's a kapo?" asked a young man standing nearby in a yellow kimono.

Everett and Shea wished their doorman a good night and Shea asked if he should hail a cab.

"Let's walk. I'm not sure I still want to go."

"I knew it. You always do this."

"Let me just think about this some more."

As they headed across town toward the East Side, Everett tried to think of polite ways of reminding the people he knew would be there that protease inhibitors were now obviously a disaster, as the dissidents had predicted. Everett had nearly been asked to leave a party when he had announced that several scientists had said that the therapeutic AIDS cocktail would turn out to be the same kind of Drano that AZT was. Everett had chronically violated AIDS activist etiquette. He was never supposed to suggest that anything was amiss where AIDS was concerned. What Everett had said about protease inhibitors had cost them an entire season of invitations to the Island. He had mischievously suggested that Socrates' death cup was actually filled with an ancient form of protease inhibitors.

"Maybe we should just talk to all of them about the weather," said Shea.

When they reached Park Avenue they still had two blocks to go, but Everett eyed a pub called Shaughnessy O'Toole's and said "Let's stop in this place and have a drink and think about this."

"We're going to arrive at this party looped. They'll have us at a disadvantage."

"Oh, they'll all be tanked. The kimonos will be half off."

Everyone at Shaughnessy O'Toole's looked at them when they walked in. It was a bar full of men who might have once been longshoremen. They were all watching a baseball game and drinking shots of some shiny brown liquor. In their expensive suits, Everett and Shea looked totally out of place. Everyone at the bar seemed to make a disapproving face when Everett ordered a vodka martini straight up with olives. Everett knew what the men were thinking, but he didn't care.

They carried their drinks to a table in the back and

the men at the bar turned their attention back to the game. The bar had an aggressive cumulus of cigarette smoke that made Shea cough. Everett looked over at the steam table which had serious slabs of ham, pastrami, and corned beef.

Everett had a feeling that the men at the bar didn't know what the gay men at the kimono party knew: that gay men are powerful and have nothing to worry about. That they have important friends. That Hollywood stars come to their AIDS benefits. That senators give them billions for their plague. That Broadway producers and gossip columnists come to their funerals. That the real centers of power in America are Cherry Grove and the Pines. That anyone who thinks the government is lying about AIDS is a nut. That when the government orders gay men to do anything medically, it is for their own good. That there will soon be an effective AIDS vaccine (there just has to be), and every gay man will show how much in love he is with his country and its trustworthy scientists by taking it, no matter what the risk, no matter what the allegations of fraud and deceit. If the heterosexual men at the bar only knew how powerful gay men are they would be clamoring to get into the kimono party.

These testy thoughts made Everett hungry. He eyed the meat on the steam table. It was gross, but he wanted to run over and grab chunks of it and stuff it into his mouth. His mood was ravenous, masculine, angry, and funky, not the kind of mood he could see in the middle of a gay kimono party.

A couple of the men at the bar stared over at Everett and Shea in a manner that demanded to know what the two of them were doing in their bar.

Every time the host went to the door to greet new guests, all the kimonos in the room turned to look for Everett and Shea. They were all the partygoers could talk about.

Most guests at the party had some bitter memory of

a confrontation with Everett from the time the epidemic began. Everett constantly made vicious fun of the AIDS activists. Everett called the AIDS benefits (which they were so proud of) "genocide parties." Everett said that the scientists who believed that HIV was not the cause of AIDS would eventually turn out to be heroes. And he was always bringing up that old bag Hannah Arendt. Always throwing her in their faces. It was a shame that he was a Hannah Arendt scholar because he could only see the epidemic through Hannah Arendt glasses. Who cared about her? Wasn't she a big closet lesbian or something? Why did he insist on turning every gay party into a seminar on that dead woman? He had no respect for any of the leading lights of the gay community who tried to talk reason to him at parties. Everett had abandoned his people at a time when they needed his loyalty and solidarity.

They were all there that night in kimonos. It was truly a powerful gay party. The man in the magenta kimono had started the biggest AIDS organization on the East Coast. The man in the gray kimono had lobbied for millions of dollars in AIDS prevention funds, money that had ended up in the coffers of hundreds of blossoming AIDS organizations. The man in the tangerine kimono had written the most important AIDS ballad, one that now tearfully closed every cabaret act in town. Beneath the other colorful kimonos in the room lay the entire infrastructure of what was referred to as "the AIDS community." At one time or another nearly every man at the party had listened in horror as Everett referred to the AIDS activist movement as "the Occupation." Everyone was asking why their beloved host had stooped to inviting Everett and Shea to the gay kimono party.

The host was frantically trying to get the party back on track. He ran around the sea of kimonos with a tray of imported caviar-topped sushi. He pressed more drinks on people and ordered the bartender to start opening the champagne. He now knew that he had made a terrible mistake by inviting Everett and Shea. He was terrified to think of what might happen when they arrived in their suits. There might be a gay *auto-da-fé*.

At O'Toole's, Everett stood up, walked over to the bar and ordered two more martinis. The bartender was polite, but a number of men at the bar skulked in his direction. He took the drinks back to the table, this time slightly spilling them. He sat down and gazed over at the old man making sandwiches behind the hot table. This was not the kind of place at which they would normally find themselves dining.

He looked at Shea and then back over at the sweating carcasses of meat and said, "Well, we're here. Let's just do it. We won't have to risk getting cheese dip all over the suits at the party if we eat first."

He walked over to the old man and asked for two corned beef sandwiches on rye. The old man was friendlier than anyone else in the place. Everett thought that it was even possible that the old man was gay.

Shea sat alone thinking it was the strangest thing that they were in this Irish bar. It was another world. Living with Everett, Shea was never sure where he was going to end up. Sometimes he felt like a refugee in his own city. The drinks had made him feel a little testy. He might just let some of the nasty queens have it between the eyes at the party if they went after Everett. He knew they thought he was some kind of yes-lover. He knew that they liked to isolate Everett and make him sound like he was the only person in the world who thought about the epidemic the way he did. They all assumed that Shea must secretly disagree with Everett, but that he was under some spell. He was thinking about his desire to move out of New York as Everett brought the working-class sized sandwiches back to the table.

"Are you man enough to eat this, Shea?"

"Are we going to arrive at the kimono party with corned beef between our teeth?" asked Shea.

The party had become a lost cause, and the host just let it go. Some people were doing impressions of Everett talking about Hannah Arendt, and some were going even further, trying to do Hannah Arendt herself.

Everywhere the host looked, people were lambasting Everett and Shea. It was as though someone had said, "Hey kids, let's put on a show for Everett and Shea about how we're building an AIDS paradigm that will get us all liquidated!"

Some of the men in kimonos were doing impressions of Hannah Arendt that sounded suspiciously like Tallulah Bankhead. There are some gay men whose every impression, even Liza Minnelli, sounds like Tallulah Bankhead.

One couldn't escape it. All around the room the satire and sarcasm were crackling. Everyone was making vicious fun of Everett's analysis of the AIDS epidemic.

"We're prepared to round everyone up, if necessary," said a gay man in an orange kimono.

A pink kimono upped the ante with, "We refuse to go outside the community for help. We demand the right to have our own gay doctors kill gay men with experimental treatments. We believe in genocide with dignity."

"I am life unworthy of life," quipped a gay man in a mummy-colored kimono.

There was one gentleman who hadn't had time to rent an authentic kimono, so he wore a large aquamarine muumuu with a belt from a bathrobe. At least he was trying to be a team player. In the spirit of the evening, he shouted out, "We're all just gay functionaries of death. We're all just gay functionaries of death."

The satire was hitting its mark. All over the room people were howling with laughter. It was getting so loud that the host began to worry about the tenants in the other apartments.

"Hannah, babe, we hope you are looking down at us tonight, us poor submissive retarded gays who are collaborating in our own demise," screamed a man in a turquoise kimono.

"Why it seems like just yesterday Hannah was saying to me that a gay man can't live an honorable life inside the AIDS community," snickered a man in a green kimono.

A man in a grey flannel kimono tried to top him with "Oh, really? Well, I was talking to her last week and she quoted Ben Gurion to me. Something about the AIDS activist movement leading to the gas chamber and the soap factory. I'm so scared."

"Go Girl!" said the man in the yellow kimono.

"Move it, everyone. Let's board the trains to the AIDS concentration camps. Don't forget to bring your AZT and your cocktails of death!" howled a man in a checkered kimono.

"Let's all go to our deaths like gay lambs to the slaughter so Everett can write learned monographs about us," said a man in a golden kimono.

The room was a kaleidoscope of laughing, out-of-control men in kimonos. The host thought it was the legendary creativity of the gay community at its best. It was the same energy that had given the world the ceiling of the Sistine Chapel, *Hello, Dolly!* and brunch.

"Come on, everyone, let's line up for the AIDS authorities and give them our names and addresses so we can show them how willing we are to participate in our own extermination," said a man in a silver kimono.

And wouldn't you know it, they did just that. They formed a long conga line that stretched through several rooms of the apartment. To the tune of "Ninety-nine Bottles of Beer on the Wall," they all began singing, "The AIDS establishment is out of its mind, the AIDS establishment is out of its mind!"—a line that they had all heard more than once from Everett.

As a veteran party giver, the host knew that this was the precise moment to distribute the tambourines. He signaled to the bartender and fifty tambourines were handed out from behind the bar, and soon the room reached a crescendo of tambourine mayhem. The whole room suddenly erupted into a festive chant, "WORK WILL SET US FREE, BLANCHE! WORK WILL SET US FREE, BLANCHE!"

If Everett and Shea had walked in at that moment, they would have been mortified. Destroyed.

One man was lifted by several others in his kimono and was whirled upon muscular arms in the air around the room and resembled the Flying Nun. People were laughing so hard they were crying. It truly had turned into the gayest party of the year.

For more than a decade of the epidemic, Everett had shown up at gay parties all over Manhattan and spoiled them. Now he was getting his just desserts. The host recognized, that true to form, the best parties are the ones where the unexpected happens. Hannah Arendt might be dead as a door nail, but she had helped to make this a party for the books. The host was grateful that he had invited Everett and Shea. And that they had not arrived.

As Shea expected, when they were done with their drinks and sandwiches, Everett said they should just skip the party and go home, that he wasn't up to a confrontation with the gay zeitgeist. As the gay pariahs left the Irish bar, there was a palpable collective sigh of relief in the dark, smoky space behind them. Their absence was welcome at more than one location in town that night.

Everett was annoyed with himself. He wondered what Hannah Arendt would say about a man who passed up an evening in which he might have turned a doomed people around. If he had argued with Hannah and insisted that there wasn't a chance, she would have said that until you are dead there is always a chance, that a man is a creature who can always start something new. Perhaps he would have finally found the right words to wake them up that evening. He tried to imagine what the party must have been like. There probably weren't any serious arguments. Not a single discomforting word would be said about the epidemic. Without Everett's contentiousness the party might have been a little boring. He wondered if the gay men in their kimonos had gone all the way, even over the top, with their costumes. Were they all there in the complete period detail that gay men were so famous for when it came to costume parties? He could imagine that some might even have gone to the trouble of having their feet bound.

The Swans

Every community has its share of evil eyes, and the gay community is no exception. And boy, were they sparkling with envy the night that Brian and Lancelot met in a small club on the east side of Manhattan.

From a political point of view, they met very, very cute. A single word brought them together, raising serious questions about the hand of destiny worthy of the Russian novelists, for if a particular word did not exist at that time and in that place, the great love which was engendered and the events that followed, might never have come into being. Perhaps it was definitive proof that beauty and grace can burst forth from the most hopeless husks of ugliness and hate, for that word, we are ashamed to say, was "queer."

If a certain inebriated man at the crowded bar had not loudly referred to himself in conversation as a "queer," Brian and Lance might have gone off into the night and the rest of their lives on unconnected paths to places far less thrilling than the ones that awaited them. In the split second that they both turned in horror and disgust to see from whence the word "queer" emanated, their eyes met and what they saw was something that would last all eternity. Perhaps if these two men had found each other under any other circumstances, they would still have fallen in love, but who knows? Perhaps the mutual scowl directed at the "queer" let them see more deeply into each other's souls. If looks could kill, the sneer that formed on Brian and Lance's faces would have taken out a small army. They both hated the word "queer" about as much as a human being can hate a word. It was the transforming magic of seeing the same look on the other's face that brought Brian and Lance together for all time.

The two men had emigrated to New York in the early Nineties from culturally distinct parts of the country. Brian had come down from the hills of New England where he had attended a small liberal arts college. He had majored in English and was determined to be a published poet one day. He had moved to New York with very little money and found his way into the kind of job most English majors end up in: He was an editorial assistant at a major publishing house. He made barely enough to support himself, but at least there was always a chance that some important literary event would take place around him.

Lance was the real butch thing. Raised on a ranch in the Lone Star State by a cowboy father and a cowgirl mother, he had one day decided that Texas was not a closet he wanted to continue living in. He began to feel like the whole state was one big angry prison with cactus and cattle. He headed off to New York City in his cowboy boots and was determined to rustle himself up a lover. Lance left the state with enough money from a grandparent's bequest to take his chances on making a living off of the stock market. Lance had good luck and it followed him to the New York Stock Exchange.

Brian and Lancelot had arrived in the city only a few months apart. Like many gay men in their twenties, visually they thought they had found the ultimate gay candy store. They had never seen so many attractive available men in one place before. But something wasn't right about most of the men. In fact, something seemed out of kilter about the whole New York gay scene. It was intangible but palpable. It had something to do with the epidemic. Everyone seemed to be wearing red ribbons. Everyone seemed to be coming from or going to doctors' offices. Everyone seemed to be telling lame, nervous jokes about condoms. And perhaps most disturbing of all, a growing number of gay men had taken to calling themselves "queers." This struck both Brian and Lance as being the same as women going around calling themselves "cunts," or blacks calling themselves "niggers," or Jews insisting on being called "kikes." Whenever Brian and Lance complained about the word, they were told that it was "no big deal." Some people told them that it was a youth culture word, and not to adopt it was to show one's age. The word's repulsiveness made Brian and Lance feel very alone in Manhattan. Neither of them could find anyone who was really disgusted by the word until the fateful night they met each other.

Like most lovers, they were bound to remember the first words they would say to each other. In this case, it was Lance who made the first move. He leaned over to Brian and whispered seductively, "What the hell is wrong with these people?"

"A bunch of dickheads," was Brian's sultry response.

It was love at first gay political analysis, and subconsciously, the whole bar was painfully aware of what was happening. Envious eyes were flashing like Christmas lights all over the room as Brian and Lance began to talk to each other in that deep intense way that implies a night of the kind of mad passionate love that would elude most of the starving men around them. It was clear that Brian and Lance were spiritually already in bed with each other. As Brian and Lance moved physically closer and closer to each other, the juices that really fuel society were flowing through the circulatory system of the bar: hostility, petulance, jealously, spite, and passive-aggression.

The denizens of the bars would have been even more distressed if they knew that it was contempt for them and their ribbons and their "queerness" that was drawing Brian and Lance so intensely to each other. Like most lovers, they were reeling from the shock that they had so much in common, but in this case it had nothing to do with the brand of vodka they ordered, the kind of music they liked, or which movies they both had seen several times. Brian and Lance were magically merging because they were both bigots. They both hated stupid people. And as they got to know each other better that night, it was clear that they both thought the gay world around them was stupid to its very core. Furthermore, they both agreed on the source. It was AIDS activism. In New York, AIDS had brought in a rich harvest of fools. Everywhere they looked there were AIDS zombies in red ribbons. In each other, Brian and Lance had found someone from the same planet.

Nothing brought Brian and Lance closer together than finding out that they both had received letters of warning from the prestigious Council on AIDS Perkiness. Both had been quickly identified by AIDS activists as slackers in the collective fight against AIDS. They had been sighted numerous times without red ribbons and there was no evidence that either of them had ever attended an AIDS dance party benefit or poetry reading. Neither of them had ever taken AIDS education posters home to hang over their beds. No one had ever seen them loading AIDS prevention tapes into their Walkmans. There were even rumors that one of them had flipped the bird at Elizabeth Taylor during one of her important television commercials about AIDS. And both of them had been exceedingly rude to AIDS counselors who had approached them in various bars.

"I tore the letter of reprimand I got from the Council on AIDS Perkiness as soon as I go it," said Brian.

"I made a dart board out of mine," said Lance.

Brian and Lance amused each other by recounting their various experiences with the AIDS Activists. Lance howled with laughter as Brian described asking one of the activists how the AIDS virus was so smart and that it knew who was gay and who wasn't. The activist was one of the brighter ones and had caught the skepticism and sarcasm of

Brian's question. In response, the AIDS activist started chanting at the top of his lungs into Brian's face, "ARE YOU SAYING THERE'S NO AIDS EPIDEMIC? ARE YOU SAYING THERE'S NO AIDS EPIDEMIC? ARE YOU SAYING THERE'S NO AIDS EPIDEMIC?"

Lance told Brian that a similar thing had happened to him when he asked an activist why everyone who had taken AZT was dead.

Throughout the rest of the evening, Brian and Lance made the bar patrons very edgy when they amused each other by saying mockingly, perhaps too loudly, "ARE YOU SAYING THAT THERE'S NO AIDS EPIDEMIC?" They seemed to the horrified onlookers not to know that early on in the epidemic one of the leading gay writers had said that nothing funny could be said or written about AIDS. They were being very bad.

When Brian and Lance finally left the bar that evening, the gay men they left behind were sending out inaudible signals from their souls that reached the four quarters of the gay world. It was a concise kind of gay Morse code. Dash-dash-dot. Two alpha males had met. Dot-dot-dash. They had instantly fallen in love. Dot-dot-dot-dash. Their love looked like a threat to Queer theorists everywhere.

Like most nights when two people have found the perfect partner, time turned romantically surreal as they arrived at Brian's apartment on upper Broadway. They both lost their chronological bearings as they began to enter each other's mysterious time zone.

The windows of Brian's bedroom suddenly opened by themselves and the curtains flung themselves back. A great wind and a blinding light filled the bedroom and both of their bodies began to writhe in an ecstasy that was so powerful and overwhelming that when they opened their eyes they were no longer human. The awesome love they had found that night had totally transformed them, for they had turned into magnificent swans.

The wind that had filled the room lifted the two swans up and before they knew it, they were swept out through the open windows and were flapping their wings side by side high above upper Broadway. Trailing streams of light the two swans began flying down Broadway. People staring out of windows in tall buildings that they passed looked on in amazement. Some people immediately surmised that this was more proof that the quality of life had improved so much in Manhattan that swans felt safe enough to return to the city.

The swans moved at such a rapid clip that they arrived at Times Square in no time at all. People who had stayed at the bars till closing hour thought that this was an indication that they had had far too much to drink. As the swans crossed 42nd Street, some late night party people looked up and wondered if this was some new promotion from the Disney folks who seemed bent on taking over the whole city, the sky included. It wasn't just the unexpected sight of swans that struck onlookers as magical but also the amazing light that surrounded them. This was a city known for its extraordinary lighting techniques, but the quality of light around the swans was a kind that no one had ever seen before.

When the swans reached 34th Street, they took the time to circle the Empire State Building several times. At the top of the structure, they left several rings of multi-colored light. People working the late shift in some of the offices thought they were seeing things. As the swans headed further downtown, they could see into the windows where people were asleep or making love. Young lovers in the act who could see the swans passing must have thought that this was some kind of divine sign that they had finally found the right person.

When the swans reached the World Trade Center, they were spotted by a freelance cameraman who worked for a local New York television news show. He immediately recognized that there was a story here. In his entire professional career he had never seen a single swan in the air over Manhattan. He started rolling his video camera as he called the station from his cell phone. The swans moved with such synchronicity and grace that he was sure that they were a couple. He knew this one would tug at heartstrings of his editor at the station. It was a good thing too, because not much else was happening in the city that night.

When Brian and Lance woke up the next morning they each had living proof in their arms that the body can satisfy the soul. Somehow in the dark and treacherous forest of AIDS activists and Queer Theorists, they had finally found happiness. Now their lives could take flight.

Everyone at Channel One News was crowing that they had been the first channel to get the swan couple. As expected, when he was interviewed about the incident, the mayor didn't know what swans the reporters were talking about, but he promptly took credit for the appearance of the swans, citing the fact that crime was down in the city, and crime was not good for swans, either. The *Post* and the *News* cheated by lifting a photo from the Channel One video for their covers. "Swan Love Couple" was the first edition headline of the *Post*. The editorial writers at the *News* jumped on the swans as a symbol of the city's rebirth. They said that this was a sign that people would soon be able to swim in the Hudson River again. The mayor had made the city safe for every living creature.

When Brian and Lance passed the newsstands on their way to work and saw the covers of all the papers, they were captivated by the images of the swans soaring above the metropolis. And they both had a sense of *déjà vu* which they traced to dreams they each had about swans the night before.

They didn't need the images of swans for

inspiration at this moment in their lives, for they were both in the middle of the long swoon that all great lovers know so well. Brian and Lance, even as they negotiated the minutia of their day, were in an altered state. They traveled through time on great waves of inner music. They were now being orchestrated by something larger than the two of them.

Lance saw Brian's face all day long at the brokerage firm. The Dow Jones turned into Brian. The Fed turned into Brian. When Bill Gates was interviewed on *Bloomberg News*, it was Brian sitting there talking about Windows 98.

Uptown in the publishing district, every character in whatever manuscript Brian was reading was competing against thoughts of Lance. When he sat in on an editorial meeting, Brian had to fight to pay attention to the various pitches the senior editors were making to the editor-in-chief. Brian knew that his chances of becoming a senior editor with a serious salary were dependent upon him looking smart at these meetings. Brian kept trying to think of some precocious, edgy, in-your-face, really cool literary wisecrack to say to the older editors to make them think that he spoke for a generation, and that the house's commercial future depended upon his taste, but all he could think about was the nature of love and the mysterious magnetism of rugged male beauty.

When one of the editors waved the *Post* with the swan cover story and started shouting, "We've got to get this first," Brian woke up from his romantic trance.

"This is going to be big," said one of the senior editors, "I can feel it. We've got to get it fast."

"I bet Binky Urban is the swans' agent," said one of the editors.

"I think my generation can really get into this," said Brian.

"Are you sure, Brian?" asked the editor-in-chief. "I

don't see much irony in this swan story."

"Well, sir, the ironic fact is that my ironic generation is really sick to death of irony."

Brian had scored a big one here. A hush came over the room as though the senior editors were in the presence of a phenomenal new literary Zen master. Around the table knowing glances were exchanged that said this kid is really going places. All eyes in the room were upon Brian's Giaconda smile which was emanating from his feeling that love increases one's intelligence, one's luck, and one's career prospects.

"So whom can we get to do this immediately?" asked the editor holding the *Post*.

"It has to be somebody big who needs the money," said the editor-in-chief.

"Well, I guess I know who that is," said another editor at the table.

"Yes," said the editor-in-chief. "Mailer."

Brian and Lance talked frequently on the phone that day. They loved the sound of each other's voice. When Brian spoke, Lance could hear the sound of citizens upholding democracy in town meetings throughout New England. He could see the determined Paul Revere racing through town squares. There was something incredibly trustworthy and solid about Brian. In Lance's voice, Brian could hear the adventure of the Great American West.

The two young men spoke to each other as though they had been together in another life. There was no doubt that they would get together that night for dinner. And the next night and every night after that.

When they met at Fedora's, a little Italian restaurant in the Village, their excitement about being with each other was obvious to the tables around them. The restaurant was filled with gay men who hailed from every era in gay life including the Pleistocene. The diners sitting next to the couple looked sheepishly into their drinks as they tried to eavesdrop, dying to hear the otherworldly small talk of eternal love. They also hoped to hear Brian and Lance say something naughty to each other.

What they heard, however, was a bit disconcerting, especially for those who were wearing red ribbons while downing their whiskey sours and eating their pasta. Brian and Lance were being drawn into a vortex of greater and greater intimacy by their shared stories of narrow political escape. These two young men were talking like they had survived some terrible secret war. Brian told Lance that he had been stalked by Queer Theorists almost from the moment that he showed up at a Manhattan gay bar for the first time. Someone had heard him referring to gay men as " gay men" rather than "queers," and they immediately knew they had a "queer men's crisis" on their hands.

When a man in his thirties approached Brian that first night with a free ticket to a Staten Island resort, Brian was a little suspicious. The man said it was the community's way of welcoming immigrants. The ticket was for a full weekend at a place called "The Queer Farm." Brian was initially impressed with the stranger's friendliness and generosity, but the name of the place worried him, so he told the man that he would postpone his visit until he had settled down in the city.

Brian told Lance that he was glad he'd followed his intuition, because in the following months he had found out the truth about the resort. The "Queer Farm" was a secret place on Staten Island for gay men who arrived in Manhattan who were in desperate need of "queer orientation." He had learned that upon arrival at the resort, visitors were given just about every recreational drug known to man.

Then, when their minds were tripping in every direction, they were taken to "queer re-education classes" inside a simulated discotheque. As the whacked-out men sat at their desks with Gloria Gaynor and Sylvester blaring loudly in the background, they were taught all the "Oh, Mary" and "Go, Girlfriend" vernacular they would need to navigate the gay bars in New York City. Then they were taught the basics of Queer Theory: the rolling of the eyes, the snap-queeniness, the perpetual whiny dismissiveness, and most importantly, how to seal oneself hermetically in an air of supercilious sniffiness. They were taught the importance of "reclaiming" all the words that had been used against gay people as their own. The primal word was of course "queer." The more times that one referred to oneself and one's friends as "queer" the better. That would have a devastating impact on society. The war for liberation was a war of words, and the more one adopted the language of the enemy, the better. If one's verbal armamentarium suffered from "queer" exhaustion, there was always "pansy," "sodomite," "fairy," or the eminently reclaimable British classic, "poofter." Aggressively calling oneself "poofter" in England was certain to bring every British homophobe to his knees. The Queer Theorists lectured the classes on the Queer Farm that this brilliant linguistic strategy had already had a profound effect upon society, that the sound of gay men referring to themselves as "queers" had completely disoriented the mainstream of America. "We're winning the language wars," boasted the Queer Theorists. The men in the classes were also taught the importance of running naked through the streets on the annual Gay Pride Day with balloons tied around their genitals. They were told that the first rule of political struggle is to get noticed, and this always worked on Gay Pride Day. It was amazing how Aristotelian the logic of all this seemed to the Queer Farm inductees who had a little Special K, cocaine, and Ecstasy in their systems. This secret resort was a very effective boot camp; thousands of young gay men left Manhattan with silly romantic dreams of love and simple political justice and returned from Staten Island as hardened, battle-ready "queers."

Lance stared into Brian's eyes and sighed an enormous sigh of relief, "What if the Queer Theorists had gotten you? We wouldn't be here tonight."

They studied each other like two men who had narrowly escaped death in a plane that had lost its hydraulic system. Lance then told Brian about the time he had eluded the AIDS activists.

"They approached me at a club with a very big offer, one they thought I couldn't refuse," said Lance.

The activists had wanted to give Lance one of the most lucrative AIDS modeling contracts in history. They had secretly taken his picture and worked up dozens of AIDS campaigns with his cowboy image. They thought they had found New York's newest AIDS stud.

"They had me sitting on a horse in an AIDS testing poster that said 'Howdy! Get tested pardner!' They had me standing against a backdrop of a stunning mountain range in an ad for AZT, with the line 'We'll climb the mountain of AIDS together.' They said I had the manly good looks that they felt promoted the proactive AIDS agenda. They even used special computer-generated techniques to show me wrestling in a field of sunflowers with a dog in an ad that said 'Man's best friend is really a condom.' And worst of all, they even had someone work up my image laid out in a casket for a gay funeral home that said 'In the end, what matters is that you look good.' "

"No way!" said Brian. He looked like he was about to cry.

"They offered me millions. Thank God I had money. Who knows what someone will do when they are down and out? I told them that if they didn't destroy the ads, I would sue every single one of them out of the activist business."

The two fell silent and their stillness was filled with mutual gratitude for whatever it is that brings souls together in the darkest of times.

They returned to Brian's apartment full of the impatience of new lovers. The lights in Brian's bedroom went off early that night, and shortly afterwards, it happened again. As soon as the two touched each other, the curtains and the windows of the bedroom spontaneously opened. Then a wind and a light of Biblical proportions swirled into the room and once again the two men turned into swans and headed out into the star-filled sky above Manhattan. This time the swans headed out into a pattern that would take them up the Hudson and around the whole island.

The last Circle Line tour of the evening was still in the water, and the passengers almost capsized the ship as they ran to the side and tried to photograph the swans with their night-vision cameras. The captain of the ship called Channel One on his cell phone, and the station broke into the news to tell New York City residents that the swans were making night flights over Manhattan again. Word spread quickly throughout the city as residents stretched out of windows to get a look at the new icons of New York's improvement in the quality of life. The streets of Manhattan quickly filled with citizens heading for the East River to catch a glimpse of the new celebrities.

A car rushed the mayor to midtown so he could stand at the United Nations to be photographed as the swans crossed the sky above him. It was an astounding passage. The light around the swans had the same otherworldly quality and it made the East River iridescent. In the sky behind the swans were sparks of gold, silver, green, and turquoise. It was an image that some of the middle-aged onlookers thought they recognized from their LSD days.

Up and down the East Side, New Yorkers cheered and applauded as the swans passed. It was better than anything that Macy's had ever put on.

The next morning the lovers awoke from their flight

in a state of nirvana. Both had very foggy memories and both said they felt like they had awakened from a sleep of a thousand years. Upon waking, both wondered what day it was and where they were. They had the weird sensation that they had just been born.

On their way to work that day, they noticed that the swans were once again on the front page of every newspaper. They both immediately identified with the swans and saw them as a symbol of their new love. The *Daily News* headline was "Swans Take City by Storm." In a similar vein, the *Post* headline was "The Swans Are the New Keys to the City." The *Times* did a page-one story about the history of swans and their potential effect on the economic life of the city. One real estate agent said the price of co-ops on high floors was bound to go up. And several travel agents said they thought the swans might double travel numbers to the already popular metropolis. The *Times* also did a sidebar on the cultural meaning of the swans. A former student of Robert Graves was quoted as saying that he thought the swans could have a major impact on the mythology of New York City. He also said that he wouldn't be surprised if unicorns and golden pigs began to roam the city in the near future.

The swans lifted the mood of the entire country. Children all over New York were as captivated by the swans as they were by stories of Santa Claus. In every elementary school drawing class, children chose swans as the favorite subjects to sketch. Illustrations and paintings of swans soon lined school hallways in all five boroughs. Adults began to talk about redemption and resurrection. Romance was in the city air. Nearly every person with a therapist brought up their feelings about the swans. Single people who saw the swans suddenly believed that there was a lover out there somewhere looking for them, that no one could be alone forever. Even a prisoner at Rikers Island who could barely make out the swans as they passed over the prison after he had been beaten to a bloody pulp (by two correction officers who were engaged in improving the city's quality of life) was captivated by the swans. He thought that God is merciful and good and that soon he would be taken to heaven by the swans.

When Brian got to his publishing house that morning, the company was in a state of crisis. One of Mailer's people had told the house that Mailer would consider the project too flaky, so they'd better try someone else. Mailer's people had suggested Vidal, but the editor-in-chief suspected that the suggestion was catty and facetious. The editors were all told to get on the phone with the city's top agents and find a high profile writer who would rush a swan bestseller into print. Brian was asked to join a small group of editorial assistants in preparing a data base on swans that could be used for background by the author once they found one. The assignment made Brian inexplicably happy.

That evening Brian and Lance met at a restaurant on the Upper East Side. They were both amused when the waitress approached their table wearing a large swan broach on her uniform.

"My grandmother gave me this," she said. "I never thought I'd be caught dead wearing it, but under the present circumstances, it's kind of cool, don't you think?"

They both agreed, and as they looked around the restaurant, it looked like every woman dining there had the same grandmother. Swan mania had gripped the entire city.

After Brian and Lance exchanged a few more stories about their close calls with Queer Theorists and AIDS activists, Brian told Lance all the interesting things he had learned at work about swans. They both became a little spacy as they discussed the swans, and once again, everyone around them at the restaurant could tell that they were in the presence of an extraordinary love.

After dinner they strolled east toward the river to

see if they could get a glimpse of the swans. Near First Avenue they encountered a familiar looking man in a black cape and beret. It was the city's leading Queer Theorist and they both shuddered when they recognized him. Lance put his arm around Brian and pulled him closer as the caped Queer Theorist passed. He gave them both a dirty look, as though he knew who they were. They suddenly felt both vulnerable and brave. They wanted to protect each other from Queer Theorists and AIDS activists and the homophobes that were chomping at the bit all over America. Their love would make them warriors.

Time passed quickly as they gazed up at the stars from their perch on the East River. It was an incredibly beautiful summer night and the sky was crystal clear. It would have been a great night to have watched the pageant of the swans. After a couple of hours, disappointed that they hadn't shown up, Brian and Lance headed back to Brian's where their new world of total erotic happiness awaited them.

Later that night, the swans were spotted flying in circles above Harlem. People danced in the streets and were convinced that this was a sign that their community might survive the city's quality of life campaign.

Entrepreneurs swiftly took advantage of the swans. All kinds of swan T-shirts were hawked on the city's streets. The few street artists who were able to escape prosecution under the city's quality of life laws were making a killing by selling paintings of the swans flying over just about every monument in New York City. Swan dolls filled the windows of the leading department stores. People dissatisfied with the politics of New York City discussed the possibility of starting a Swan Party to challenge the hegemony of the Democrats and the Republicans.

Every night as Brian and Lance's relationship became more and more intense, the flights of the swans became more and more dazzling and inventive.

Choreographers at Lincoln Center began incorporating some of the more unique movements executed by the swans into their dances. NBC considered updating its logo from a peacock to a swan.

The flights of the swans were such a widely anticipated nocturnal event that the Gray Line scheduled special buses that followed the flight of the birds every night. The swans soon became the number-one worldwide attraction. They seemed to quench some international thirst for transcendence and harmony.

Not everyone had the same feelings of wonder and joy about the swans. On a small farm outside of New Hope, Pennsylvania, a retired zoologist was not at all captivated by the swans. Perhaps the man had had a bad swan experience in his past, or he just lacked imagination; whatever it was, the zoologist thought that there was something weird about a city that was so obsessed by a couple of birds. He was a cranky man and he had a rather unpleasant idea about the swans that he wanted to check out.

One Friday night he drove his wife into the city for a steak dinner and afterwards they hailed a cab to take them to the promenade on the Upper East Side near the river. Luckily, Brian and Lance had turned in early that evening, so the zoologist and his wife did not have to wait until the middle of the night for what the zoologist wanted to see. When the swans approached in all of their glory, the zoologist and his wife could hear the sound of cheers and applause up and down the river's promenade. The zoologist's wife was transfixed by the sight. For some reason it reminded her of the night after their wedding. She was hoping her husband would put his arm around her. But her husband was busily examining the two celebrated swans through giant infrared binoculars he had brought with him.

"Ah ha! Just what I thought! Why hasn't anyone noticed this?" he exclaimed.

"Let me look," his wife said. "What do you see?"

"They're male. It's a male couple!" he shouted.

"They're gay?" she asked.

"What do you expect? It's Manhattan."

As soon as the couple arrived back in New Hope, the husband went to the computer and e-mailed the *New York Post*.

It didn't take long for the swan story to take a new, even more sensational direction. The *Post* ran a cover picture of the swans with the headline "Gay As Geese?"

The *Times* waited until experts could be contacted in Washington before reporting the fact that the swans were a gay couple. While some in the city were delighted by the revelation, many were horrified. Parents who had urged their children to adopt the swans as role models tried to keep the tabloids away from their children. Some tried to reignite their children's interest in Lamb Chop and Barney. Images of swans were soon banned from school hallways. Several high school productions of Swan Lake were promptly cancelled.

All of a sudden, the mayor was evading questions about the swans during his press conferences. In a complete about-face, some of his staff began to suggest that the swans might actually be threatening the quality of life in New York by taking people's attention away from more important issues like jaywalking and the dangers of letting poor people clean windshields. Some conservatives in the city blamed the swans on the mayor's support of the gay community and they pointed to the legislation that the mayor had passed which urged gay couples to register with the city. One smart-alecky columnist suggested that the next thing that would happen in the city would be for the horses that pulled the carriages in front of the Plaza to all go gay.

Queer Theorists saw a great opportunity here and started a letter-writing campaign to the media urging them to refer to the swans as "queers" rather than gay. The media was only too happy to comply. As graffiti artists began to scribble "The Swans are Fags" on surfaces all over the city, the Queer Theorists countered by crossing out the word "fags" and replacing it with "queers." They were going to turn the attacks on the swans into a defining moment for Queer Theory.

Some lesbian feminists were of course a little annoyed with all the attention the male swans were getting. This was another example of white gay male media supremacy.

The AIDS activists immediately saw their own opportunity. They began incorporating the swans in their posters which said "Get tested, if you want to fly right." They were desperate to figure out how to get the swans to wear red ribbons and condoms in flight. They encouraged pharmaceutical companies to use swans in all of their ads that urged gay men to take toxic medications to bolster their immune systems.

Even in Washington the revelation about the swans' sexual orientation did not go unnoticed. One congressman was immediately attacked when he referred to the New York swans as "homos" on a right-wing radio talk show. Another congressman called the swans "flying three-dollar bills." One legislator noted on the floor of the house that the swans might not be covered by the Defense of Marriage Act, and new legislation might be called for. Nearly every conservative in Congress found some euphemistic way to deride the gay swan lifestyle.

As many in the city began to turn against the swans, Brian and Lance watched on in horror. They wished that the swans would just fly away for their own safety. They had a premonition of what was coming.

Whatever else New York City is, it is a paradise for

guns and hollow bullets. Within a few evenings of the announcement that the swans were gay, snipers were taking all kinds of pot shots at the swans. The mayor quickly warned that it was against the law to shoot any bird in the city, even a pigeon, but that didn't matter. There was something inside a number of people that had to be expressed no matter what the laws.

Soon the papers were reporting on the fact that gun shots were disturbing the sleep of many New Yorkers every night. It had become an unofficial competition: Who could kill the swans first? One militia group out west even offered a reward to anyone who could kill the gay swans. This alarmed the city's public health department because they wanted to test the swans for AIDS before anyone laid a hand on them.

It had seemed to Brian and Lance that with the gay world awash in AIDS activism and Queer Theory, that things could not get any darker. And yet somehow the swans were making the situation for gays even worse. They dreaded the morning that they would wake up and read in the papers that the swans had been successfully assassinated by some deranged sharpshooter.

But the amazing development was that no one could kill the swans. The bullets seemed literally to deliquesce instantly in the air when they got close to the swans. There was something totally protective about the light that surrounded them. In many cases, the gunmen felt something akin to a spiritual conversion when they saw their bullets vaporize in mid-air. As the bullets were swallowed by a strange protective light around the swans, the gunmen suddenly realized that they were violating some basic law of the universe. They were trying to destroy something that was operating at another level of being. The guilt that many of the would-be assassins felt caused them to reform their lives instantly. Some turned themselves into the police. They all got rid of their guns. A few decided to volunteer to help out in the city's literacy program.

Outside the city, the hate for the swans was growing like a malignant cancer. All over the country dead swans were found floating in ponds with their beautiful necks broken by fear and loathing. Every kind of swan was getting it in the neck; not just gay swans, but bisexual swans, straight swans, monogamous swans, and celibate swans. Even grandmother swans. It was a terrible time to be a swan. Crazed people who couldn't find swans turned to ducks. All across America, just having wings became a mortal liability.

The hate for the swans knew no borders. Overseas where clerical fascism was already growing at a rapid clip, the swans became a symbol of America's decadence. Some religious leaders of foreign countries demanded public executions of swans as a way of saying "Death To America!" All of this escalated the swans into a national security threat to the United States. There were some in the most secret enclaves of the national security operation in Washington who thought that, given the increase of the tensions about terrorism all over the world, it would not be a bad thing for the gay swans to just, shall we say, disappear.

An elite group of defense experts was sent to New York City to see what could be done to remove the gay swan threat to the nation. They knew that New Yorkers would never support an overt military invasion of New York City, especially since so many New Yorkers were enthralled by the swans. Something covert needed to be tried that would not get all the noisy liberals in the city up in arms. This was the perfect opportunity to try out the Defense Department's microstealth bombers, aircraft that were so small that two hundred of them could fit on the head of a pin. Needless to say, at a billion dollars apiece, this was not a weapon to fool around with.

A microstealth bomber was programmed by

operators at Fort Benning, Georgia, and late one night, the nearly invisible dust-particle-sized bomber headed for Manhattan. It might as well have been heading into a black hole in space, for when it got within inches of the swans, it disappeared from the military's top secret stealth microradar and, like the bullets, seemed to vanish into nothingness. An emergency meeting of the Joint Chiefs of Staff determined that America's super-secret, black box, mythological anti-personnel weaponry division be called in. This was a relatively new division of America's secret defense operation. It had been formed in the wake of the men's mythopoetic movement, at a time when people like Joseph Campbell and Robert Bly were being recognized as potential threats to the national mythology. Unfortunately, the mythological weapons under development were nowhere ready for deployment. It would be another decade before the advanced laser technology that could instantly burn homoerotic archetypes out of the human psyche would even be ready for testing on gay prisoners.

Keenly aware of what was going on in society, these were truly the darkest of times for Brian and Lance. But they were also the very best of times because they were together, and like the swans, they seemed to be surrounded by a light that protected them from everything. Little did they know what their love had launched into the skies above the City of New York each night as they fell into each other's arms.

They spent less and less time in the gay bars because, more and more, the AIDS activists and the Queer Theorists seemed to be winning the war for the hearts and minds of the gay community. And it came as no big surprise to them that the gay swans had become a brass ring for terrorists all over the world. They wouldn't have blinked if they had seen what was happening one night that autumn on the Lower East Side of Manhattan.

In an empty lot on Avenue A which was filled with

all kinds of garbage, there was an old piece of luggage that was unremarkable except for the fact that it contained a small nuclear weapon set to go off in the middle of the night. The device had been left there by terrorists who supported these five traditional methods of dealing with gay creatures:

1) beheading with a sword;
2) chopping in two with a sword;
3) stoning to death;
4) burning at the stake;
5) throwing alive from a mountain top or a high building.

To those five ingenious methods of punishment was about to be added a brand new contemporary one:

6) blowing up the city they're in with a nuclear bomb.

That night, when Brian and Lance retired, they held each other so tightly you would have thought it was the last time they were ever going to see each other.

Later that night, there were the usual number of curious tourists and fans of the swans awaiting their nocturnal flight along the East River. As usual, there were also a couple of foolish assassins with high powered rifles fruitlessly trying to pull an Oswald as the swans passed overhead trailing more gold and silver sparks than ever. Below them on the bank of the East River stood a couple of protesters with hand painted signs that said "God Hates Fag Swans" and "Death to all Gay and Bisexual Swans."

There was a collective gasp among the onlookers up and down the river when, for the first time they saw the regal swans suddenly descend from the sky into downtown Manhattan. Had one of the vicious anti-gay assassins finally hit their target? An ominous chill swept through the crowds congregated along the East River. There was soon, however, a giant cheer of relief when the swans ascended from the East Side again. But instead of continuing their usual flight pattern around Manhattan, the swans headed east, straight out to sea. New York One had a camera in the area and they caught the swans as they turned into a single dot of light over the ocean in the east. A reporter for one of the tabloids had a powerful telescopic camera and he was able to catch one final clear image of their exodus. One of the swans had its bill firmly clamped around the handle of a suitcase. This image caused no small amount of mirth at the paper where they crafted the headline "DID THE SWANS PACK THEIR BAGS AND LEAVE IN A GAY HUFF?"

What may have looked like a "gay huff" to Manhattanites was registering as something a little more serious in the war room of the Pentagon. Any time there is a major release of radiation detected anywhere on the earth's surface, even in the middle of the Atlantic Ocean, it is taken as a very serious threat to the United States. That the mysterious radiation incident took place the same evening that the gay Manhattan swans were reported to have departed the city for Europe was not lost on some of the finer minds in our Defense Department.

When neither Brian nor Lance showed up for work the next day there was not a great deal of concern until the late afternoon, when fellow employees began calling their apartments and continually got their answering machines. Those who were gay in their respective businesses expected the worst, because violence against gays had been increasing dramatically in the city, especially in light of the swan flights.

That night, nearly a million people disobeyed the mayor's request that they stay away from the East River. The police were worried about crowd control, but the people would not be stopped. They waited into the early morning hours, but there were no swans to be seen. Night after night people returned, but the crowds dwindled to a faithful few who were practically starting a new religion with swans as the messianic center.

The mayor of course was not unhappy to see the swans disappear from the city's skies. He chalked it all up as another victory for his quality of life in New York, little knowing that the swans had saved something more important than the quality of life in New York, namely New York itself.

Pictures of Brian and Lance started showing up as missing. The usual battery of rumors started: They had both secretly died of AIDS. They had both headed south to become ex-gays. They had admitted they couldn't make it in the Big Apple and had moved back home.

Needless to say, the Queer Theorists and the AIDS activists were not exactly in a state of mourning. They took special delight in seeing these words printed above Brian and Lance's pictures: "Have you seen these missing Queers?"

Not a trace of Brian and Lance was ever found. That is, unless you count the one perfect white feather that washed up in the surf off of Fire Island. The young man who was lucky enough to pick it out of the ocean was suddenly surrounded by light when he touched the feather. It endowed him with the vision and bravery that enabled him to save the gay community during its darkest hour, but that is another story.

Charles Ortleb was one of the most controversial journalists and publishers during the first two decades of the AIDS epidemic. From 1981 until 1997, Charles Ortleb was the Publisher and Editor-in-Chief of *New York Native*, described in Wikipedia as "the only gay paper in New York during the early part of the AIDS epidemic" which "pioneered reporting on the AIDS epidemic when others ignored it." In his bestseller, *And the Band Played On*, Randy Shilts described the *New York Native* coverage of the epidemic as being "singularly thorough" and "voluminous." In *Rolling Stone*, David Black said that *New York Native* deserved a Pulitzer Prize for its AIDS coverage. In an interview in *New York Press*, Nicholas Regush, a producer for ABC News and a reporter for *Montreal Gazette*, said that *New York Native* did "an astounding job" in its coverage of AIDS and credited it with "educating him early on." In a profile titled "The Outsider" in *Rolling Stone* in 1988, Katie Leishman wrote that "It is undeniable that many major AIDS stories were Ortleb's months and sometimes years before mainstream journalists took them up. Behind the scenes he exercises an enormous unacknowledged influence on the coverage of the medical story of the century."